The starlit night was full of promise

Luke gazed down at Jessica, who lay naked beside him. "I wanted to make love to you the first time I saw you—on the show."

"And I wanted to throttle you," she said with a laugh, looking up adoringly at the man who'd filled her life with magic.

"And now?" he murmured in a husky voice, caressing her taut nipple with his forefinger.

Jessica felt a warm melting sensation flow through her entire being. "I think *your* idea is much, much better. . . ."

THE AUTHOR

Madeline Harper is a pseudonym for the writing team of Shannon Harper and Madeline Porter. Their partnership began in 1975, and together they have coauthored ten books—no mean feat considering Madeline lives in California and Shannon in Georgia! The authors tell us they work by mail and telephone. Shannon formulates the plot and characters and then Madeline fills in the details and description. This highly successful duo also write as Anna James.

Every Intimate Detail

MADELINE HARPER

Harlequin Books

TORONTO • NEW YORK • LONDON
AMSTERDAM • PARIS • SYDNEY • HAMBURG
STOCKHOLM • ATHENS • TOKYO • MILAN

With thanks—to all the friends who helped.

Published October 1984

ISBN 0-373-25132-7

Printed in Canada

1

Jessica Hale was seething under the relentless television lights, but it wasn't the glare that caused her distress; it wasn't even the heat. It was Luke Maxwell.

She watched through narrowed slate-blue eyes as the popular host of the interview show "Speak Out" considered his next question. He stood between Jessica and the crowded studio audience, a look of studied concern on his handsome face. Jessica took a deep breath and managed to maintain an appearance that was cool and collected. But she was on trial here and she knew it; Luke Maxwell was her inquisitor—and her judge.

Her calm outward manner persisted and gave no hint of the fury within. She glowed for the TV cameras, which were so often unkind—washing out, hardening, even distorting the most pleasant face carefully prepared for the onslaught of the camera and its klieg lights, but those hot harsh white lights feebled when they caught Jessica's glow. They shimmered through her dark brown hair, caressed her radiant skin, danced on her green silk dress. They brightened her eyes and enhanced her already rare beauty. But they didn't soften the seething within.

Jessica was sitting in a modular chair onstage. The

chair beside her remained empty while Luke Maxwell, microphone in hand, roamed the aisles of the studio audience. He commanded the poise of a seasoned veteran, although his show had been on air less than two years. Nationally known, he had the reputation of a man who wasn't afraid to ask the toughest questions. Politicians, tycoons, artists, authors—he took them all on in his determinedly honest show. And now it was Jessica's turn.

"Isn't it true—" he asked, stopping in the middle of the aisle to look back at Jessica "—that you were once Crawford Dillon's protégée and that he bypassed well-qualified executives in his organization to place you in charge of Modern Times Enterprises?"

Jessica's irritation turned to barely controlled anger. She'd come on the show to talk about Modern Times and its new image, not to dredge up old gossip about her personal life, but Luke Maxwell wasn't cooperating. Behind the horn-rimmed glasses his intense brown eyes sparked with genuine interest. He paused for her answer.

Jessica's mind raced. She'd have to turn the line of questioning to her advantage, and that wasn't going to be easy. She could lead boardroom discussions, control staff meetings, handle recalcitrant advertisers and uncooperative suppliers, but this was a nationwide TV show. She was up against a studio and hometown audience loyal to Luke Maxwell. And Luke Maxwell was a pro.

Jessica spoke with calm deliberateness, as if addressing a child. She wanted every word to be understood; she wanted no stumbling blocks. "In the first place, I'm very well qualified, Mr. Maxwell—if not by seniority, certainly by interest and education." She tried to smile away the self-assured emphasis of her words, but the smile barely curved the corners of her mouth. "I've been involved with Modern Times since I was a child and groomed for the presidency since I was seventeen."

She went on to explain that her father had been Crawford Dillon's lawyer and closest friend, and when Dillon's son had been killed in a tragic accident, she'd become his protégée. Jessica didn't bother to add that when her own widower father died, she'd gone to live in the New Orleans mansion belonging to Crawford Dillon. The audience knew that. They'd read about it for years in the press, and Jessica was well aware of the rumors that had persisted about her relationship with Crawford. Only she knew the facts. She'd grown up almost as his child. When she was very young, he'd been like a father to her; by the time she was seventeen, he'd become her mentor. But she wasn't about to explain all that again.

Luke Maxwell pushed his glasses up on the bridge of his nose, ran his hand through thick russet hair in a gesture familiar to millions of viewers, and looked at Jessica thoughtfully. He registered her image almost subliminally, discovering again her dark blue eyes, her sable hair and svelte body packed into the clinging silk dress. She was a beautiful woman, and she was bright, smart enough to be a responsive guest and give him a good show.

She wasn't at all as he'd thought—a woman who'd used her connections to take over a job for which she wasn't qualified. He'd been all wrong about that. Luke wished now he'd had more time to go over the research files his assistants had prepared on Jessica Hale; he definitely wanted to know more about her. But this curiosity wouldn't keep him from his task; neither would her charm. He conducted a hard-driving interview, not a public-relations talk show. Still, his eyes rested on her a moment longer than he intended before he forced himself to look away.

Trailing the microphone cord, he moved in an arc around the studio, followed closely by two cameras. At least one cameraman always focused on him, anticipating his every move. The other sometimes panned the audience for responses or zoomed in on his guests.

As Luke walked back toward her, Jessica watched, momentarily fascinated. He moved with the animal grace of a man who'd spent time out-of-doors, in the woods and fields, the rivers and streams of a more rugged environment. Confused, Jessica shook her head and tried to return her concentration to the issue. He was standing just a few feet from her, and for a brief instant their eyes met and locked.

In the control room the director shouted to the cameraman. "Move back for a two shot. Move back!" But it was too late. The moment passed. Jessica looked away and Luke returned his attention to his notes.

"You're an intelligent woman, Ms Hale." His voice held sincere respect for her accomplishments. "You have an MBA from Harvard." He turned toward the audience to smile and tilted his head in Jessica's direction. "Smart lady. That's a tough school. Hard to get into."

Jessica allowed her defenses to drop a little at the compliment. She was proud of her background and education. Her training had given her the skill to implement important changes at MT where she'd plunged right into revision of *Modern Times* magazine, once known principally for pinups, cartoons and male-oriented articles. She was trying to make the magazine relative to both men and women, and that's what she wanted to discuss with the audience of "Speak Out." Maybe now she would get the chance.

Luke's question was preceded by a disarming smile, and before his query was even spoken, Jessica knew she was in trouble.

"With your education and intelligence, Ms Hale, you still continue to portray women as sex objects in the most popular of MT's magazines. I find that hard to understand. Maybe you can enlighten me."

He was referring to the magazine's centerfold, and for the first time Jessica showed her anger. It was obvious to Luke, and since camera number two held her in extreme close-up, the television audience would see it too. She didn't care. The first half hour of the show had been devoted to scrutinizing her personal life and now, covertly and cleverly, he brought up the centerfold, a subject that always raised her defenses.

Quickly, before Luke could add anything more to his vaguely vitriolic remark, Jessica spoke, looking away from him, into the audience. She ignored his reference to the centerfold. It was a popular staple of the magazine, and more time would have to pass before she could convince the management that it should be dropped.

Instead she talked about what *had* happened at *Modern Times*. "I've changed the focus of the magazine. We've added poetry and prose by distinguished writers. We've replaced some of our more scandalous personality pieces with in-depth interviews." She emphasized "in-depth," then cast a covert look at Luke Maxwell. He smiled blandly back at her but didn't interrupt.

"Our interviews are with international figures in business, politics and the arts. We have a top-notch staff of writers and editors. We're hoping to woo and win a different kind of audience—both men and women." She went on to explain that she believed the kinds of changes she had in mind would eventually affect the whole corporate structure of the MT empire.

Luke had kept quiet, giving her time to make her point, and she'd done it well, he thought. She'd presented a concise, well-organized outline of what she hoped *Modern Times* could become, but unfortunately speeches—no matter how well thought out—didn't make good television. Dissent did. It was time he broke in with a question, one that would make her think on her feet. She was damned good at that.

"And just what is your timetable for this change, Ms Hale? Haven't you been in charge at MT several years?"

Her blue eyes snapped as they accosted him across the studio. "All change takes time, Mr. Maxwell," she reminded him, "especially in a structure as large and far-flung as MT, but that doesn't mean it won't happen—eventually. I am committed," she went on firmly, "to making our magazine, *Modern Times*, a viable form of expression not only for the modern male but also for today's female."

Luke raised one eyebrow at that. Jessica had heard he supported women's issues but apparently only those that brought changes overnight. She went on undaunted while Luke took time to appraise her again—from her high-heeled sandals to her shining sable hair. A smile played around his mouth and danced in his dark eyes. His next question was only peripherally related to what she'd said.

"And do you consider yourself an example of the new *Modern Times* female?" Before she could reply, Luke answered for her. "*I'd* certainly say she's a modern woman—intelligent, well-educated.... But she's also sexy. Sexy enough to model in her own magazine, and she certainly doesn't try to hide it. None of those gray flannel suits for Ms Hale." The audience tittered inappropriately, but his next remark was one Jessica might have made herself had she been given the chance. "However, the modern woman—as I understand her—seems to have the confidence not to hide her sexuality."

Jessica glanced at Luke questioningly, wondering if he was about to change his opinion of her. Maybe....

Luke shrugged and looked into the audience.

"Well, let's hear what America has to say about this modern, intelligent—and very sexy woman."

Jessica sighed. No chance this man would change.

"Come on. Speak out. The lines are open, the mike's on. Let's hear from you."

After having waited patiently through the dialogue between Jessica and Luke, the audience came to life. Many of their remarks about *Modern Times* recalled the era before Jessica took over. Half a dozen times she had to remind them that she'd toned down the scandalous aspects of the magazine and that in her first week she'd killed the logo: *Modern Times*, The Magazine for Men.

She was almost saved by one question, a scornful demand that she explain what possible reason she, or any woman, could have for running a large corporation. Jessica brightened as she responded with the hope that one day a woman would head up IBM or General Motors "and certainly take up residence in the White House—and not as First Lady." She was rewarded with enthusiastic applause from more than half the audience, and she couldn't resist tossing her head a little triumphantly. If Luke Maxwell wouldn't give her an opportunity to discuss her own plans for *Modern Times*, at least now they could have a good dialogue about a woman's place in business. Jessica's eyes flashed, waiting for the next question.

It would be a long time before she let go of the belief that Luke chose the woman squeezed into the pink pantsuit intentionally.

The woman stood up, beaming, her gray hair blued a shade beyond the possible, her generous frame barely contained by the polyester outfit. She leaned toward the microphone and lowered her voice conspiratorially. "I thought it was just shameful when Miss Hale went to live with Crawford Dillon. I used to see their pictures in the paper. Why, she was no more than a child."

Luke answered for Jessica. "I think Ms Hale has adequately explained that relationship."

He could hardly have responded otherwise to that absurdity, Jessica thought, but his response was too little—and much too late.

The woman made another try at the mike. "A young girl like that—and an old man."

Jessica almost laughed. The remarks were harmless at this point in her career, so the suppressed laughter was for Crawford, who at fifty-five showed no signs of slowing down and never gave a thought to old age; in fact, growing old was a possibility he'd never even considered.

As the pink lady tried valiantly to get in another comment, she was interrupted by Luke. It was time for the two-minute break in the taping. In the control booth the director flipped off the switches and smiled. He was pleased. On the studio floor below, Luke put down his mike and frowned. He seemed puzzled. In her chair in the middle of the stage, Jessica took a grateful sip from a glass of water offered by the production assistant and wondered for the thousandth time why she'd agreed to appear on this show.

Her staff's words rang hollowly in her ears. "He's hot; he's controversial; he's a winner. It's a great forum for Modern Times. Think of the publicity!"

Grimly she handed the glass back to the waiting

assistant. She was getting publicity all right, guaranteed to tear down the careful image she'd been struggling to build during the past two years. Crawford had always been there to guide her, but most of the decisions about Modern Times Enterprises had been her own: a day-care center at the corporate headquarters; the development of coed fitness centers; a training program to advance women within the corporation; the establishment of a women's resource center; a recruitment program within the local schools and a myriad of plans for her favorite project, *Modern Times* magazine.

Granted, she'd been exposed to gossip and criticism along the way, but she'd thought that was all in the past, as if by hard work and determined professionalism Jessica had proven her competence and seriousness. Maybe she'd relaxed too much, confident that she'd been victorious over the critics. Obviously she hadn't won over Luke Maxwell. To him—and his audience—*Modern Times* continued to be nothing more than a girlie magazine and Jessica's corporation a purveyor of eroticism.

Luke's questions had left little room for her accomplishments. For a moment she wished the tables were turned and she could trade places with Luke, impaling him on the sharp edge of her questions.

Just before the taping resumed, Jessica glanced unintentionally in Luke's direction to find that he was looking at her with a quizzical expression she couldn't interpret. She wondered again if he'd begun to believe her. But as he moved back into the audience, giving his mike to eager participants in what had become a battle against Jessica Hale, it was obvious that the direction of the show had been established. There was no turning back, and during the last fifteen minutes Jessica could only try to pick up some pieces.

But no topic was sacred as the questions were asked without remorse or embarrassment. Some she answered monosyllabically, refusing to honor them with thoughtful responses. Other questions that appeared more interesting and intelligent she struggled to answer fully, but the time had long passed when anything more than a defense of her position was possible.

At last the end was near. Time for one more question from the audience. From a sea of waving hands, Maxwell chose a man, one of the few in the studio.

"What about *your* love affairs, Miss Hale? How does your philosophy at Modern Times carry over into your personal life?"

Jessica heard the leer in the man's voice. If she'd seen the look in his eyes—caught by the alert director—she might not have been able to control the urge to snap back that her personal life was no one's business but her own. Since she didn't glance at the monitor, Jessica missed the maligning look and framed a careful response. The show was almost over. She wasn't about to blow it now.

"I work seven days a week, twelve hours a day. That doesn't leave much time for a personal life." She grabbed again for the point she'd tried to make throughout the whole program. "MT is the most important part of my life. I believe in the company, and

I hope to make changes that will reflect the great future that lies ahead for *Modern Times*. The kinds of changes I foresee—"

Luke left the audience and headed back toward the set, interrupting Jessica with a warning that they were running out of time. By now the show had gone well over an hour. His brown eyes looked deeply into her blue ones, and this time the director framed the shot to perfection as Luke asked with what seemed serious interest, "Any final words to fill up these last few seconds, Ms Hale?"

Jessica paused to gather her thoughts, not about to trust the look on Luke Maxwell's face. The facts were clear—he'd used "Speak Out" to make a mockery of her. She had an answer for him all right, and it was bold if not wise.

"Only surprise, Mr. Maxwell, that the questions you asked me were so shallow."

Anger flashed in Luke's eyes, followed by amusement and then a kind of admiration. He liked her spirit and her style, but he was not about to be bested by a guest—especially in the closing seconds of the show, and so he glibly answered, turning Jessica's own words on her, "Perhaps the shallowness you refer to, Ms Hale, is in the subject matter."

Jessica opened her mouth to respond, but it was too late. The show was over. Luke smiled and turned away as the credits began to roll on the monitor. The audience noisily filed out of the studio.

Jessica sat immobile in her place of honor—the comfortable beige modular chair, which had been a seat of execution—trying to wish away the last remark. It was almost as if Luke had read her anger, set her up and then let her make a fool of herself. In trying to put him down, she'd given him the last word.

The studio emptied and Jessica got up silently, retrieved her briefcase and waved away a lurking photographer. She was in no mood to give another interview or have her photo taken. As she headed for the exit, the private emotions of Jessica Hale, public figure, began to surface. She was off the air and almost out of the studio; now she could give vent to those feelings. And she did. Jessica was livid, appalled by Luke Maxwell, his rudeness and bias. She'd heard he was honest, forthright, spending long hours on research, getting to know his guests before they appeared on "Speak Out." Obviously, someone was misinformed. Arch Wheeler, Luke's boss and owner of Wheeler Broadcasting System, was regarded as one of the most upstanding and moral men in broadcasting. He'd started the TV station to reflect his own concept of journalistic integrity. Wheeler's protégé, Jessica mused, hadn't picked up any of his mentor's finer points of moral consciousness.

Above the heavy metal door at the back of the studio a green light flashed, indicating that taping was over and all the exits were unlocked. Avoiding the heavy cables strewn across the wooden floor, Jessica made her way toward the green light through the straggle of crew members left behind to take down the set.

A voice called to her. "Ms Hale. Wait a minute, please."

Jessica turned to see Luke Maxwell approaching with a look on his face of open cordiality that gave no indication of the hour they'd just spent locked in verbal combat. He had monumental nerve, Jessica decided, to attempt overtures of friendship at this juncture. Curious, she stopped and waited for him.

Luke had taken off his jacket, loosened his tie and rolled up his shirt-sleeves to expose well-muscled, tanned forearms. Jessica was surprised that she noticed, but she did. He was tall and lean, towering above her, his after-shave crisp and clean and very masculine, but no less so than the man himself. She was reminded again of the great outdoors. She couldn't shake that image even in her barely controlled anger.

He smiled again, cunningly, she thought, and the image retreated to be replaced by her memory of the previous hour's indignity suffered at Luke Maxwell's hands.

"You're cool under pressure," he observed, looking down at her from a height of six feet two inches or more. "I admire that. Sorry I had to be so rough, but I figured you could take it. And you did. After all," he continued calmly and in a curiously intimate tone of voice, "that's what makes a good show—a certain tension between host and guest. Nothing personal."

Jessica stood looking at him, her eyes locked in concentration on his face, her expression frozen in disbelief at his peculiar explanation of what constituted a good show.

This time his ingenuous smile brightened not only his lips but his eyes. "Why don't we have dinner? I'd like to hear more about Modern Times. Maybe we can touch on some of the points we didn't have time to cover on the air." The look persisted, and it was calculated if not to melt the snows of Antarctica at least to wipe the cold mask of distaste from Jessica's face.

For once Luke Maxwell had calculated wrongly.

Jessica didn't answer at once. She just looked up at him, analyzing the deep brown eyes, the glasses that gave him the appearance of a naughty professor—and the smile. It was all wasted on her, all that boyish charm and charisma, when she remembered what had just taken place. She'd been raked over the coals by Luke, her private life held up to public scorn and her professional life demeaned—all for the sake of ratings. She wasn't about to have dinner with Luke Maxwell—now or ever.

He stood waiting, incalculably self-assured, with that sexy little half smile still lingering on his lips.

At the back of the studio the lone photographer was still hanging around, hoping for something to happen. Jessica caught the man's eye, threw him a glance that intimated something was indeed about to happen, and raised her head in a way that made him lift his camera and move in closer. When he was close enough, Jessica gave Luke her answer in a voice that carried easily to the photographer.

"Dinner, Mr. Maxwell? No thank you. You may not know the meaning of integrity, but I do. When I dine, I dine with friends."

The camera snapped, catching not only the look of contempt on Jessica's face but the stunned expression on Luke's. Knowing that the photographer's shutter was still clicking, she spun around on her three-inch heels and stalked grandly across the floor toward the metal door. The crew members parted like the Red Sea waters as Jessica made her way out of the Wheeler Broadcasting studio. She pushed through the door, let it close heavily behind her and then leaned against it for a moment. Her heart was pounding from the confrontation but it was a pounding of exultation. She'd given Luke Maxwell what he deserved. He'd think twice about humiliating her again.

2

SEVERAL MINUTES LATER Jessica eased her pale yellow Jaguar out of the WBS parking deck and rolled down the window to let in spring. It was a glorious day in April, that most magical of months, stretching between the fierce rains of winter and the interminable heat of summer. All over the city oleanders were putting out their first tentative buds, azaleas opening to the gentle sun and filling the air with the sweet scent of spring. But here on Canal Street the heavy traffic, barely inching along, added its unpleasant fumes to corrupt the fragrant morning air.

Jessica sighed. She was in no mood for spring anyway, not interested in bright sun and blue sky. If she'd glanced in the mirror she wouldn't have been particularly surprised to see a pout forming on her lips.

The cabbie who pulled up next to her noticed both Jessica and the pout.

"Cheer up, Jessica," he sang out through the wide open window. "It's a beautiful day!"

Jessica shook her head incredulously and flashed the cabbie her widest smile. The light changed, he drove off with a happy grin and Jessica almost laughed. It still amazed her that she was so often recognized, but she was the bright and beautiful New Orleans golden girl, and even those who criticized her boasted about her. She was their prize, even if they didn't always approve. Jessica had taken a lot of hard knocks since she chose to place her own spiked heels tentatively into the footsteps left at MT Enterprises by Crawford Dillon.

At first no one—except Crawford—had believed she could do it. She was too young, too inexperienced, too decidedly feminine. In fact, her femininity was an asset, she was far from inexperienced and her youth was often an advantage; besides, her years belied her worth, for Jessica had been brought up on Modern Times, first under the auspices of her father and then under the tutelage of Crawford Dillon. She'd managed the restaurants, run the casinos and opened a chain of health clubs before she even considered taking the reins of the whole corporation from Crawford, and when, at twenty-seven, Jessica walked through the doors as president of MT Enterprises, she was ready.

Not everyone thought so. Her critics didn't spare her because she was Crawford's personal choice; in fact, they sharpened their fangs on that bit of boardroom gossip. Even those who knew Crawford well— and few did, although many believed they did— bristled when he made it official: Jessica Hale, President, Modern Times Enterprises.

The first days were easy; everyone was polite. The next months were hell. She survived, and she didn't let it get her down. Then two years later, having weathered it all, she let Luke Maxwell get her down.

Jessica was angry because she'd been duped. She'd understood the interview was to be based on her new directions for MT; instead it had been a rehash of the same tired old stories, and she hadn't even been able to handle her final jab at the end of the show. That, too, had backfired on her.

The longer Jessica sat in traffic, the angrier she became at herself for being placed in such a compromising position, but more than that, at Luke Maxwell for exploiting her. He hadn't done his homework; he hadn't even tried to understand what MT was all about. And somehow—how, Jessica would never figure out—he'd managed to stir both the right and left against her.

A delivery van tried to cut in front of the Jag, and Jessica obstinately refused to make room for him. The driver's mouth formed around a probable stream of obscenities before he recognized her and stopped himself with a broad smile and a tip of his hat. Jessica shrugged and smiled back. What could she do? They loved her even while they criticized.

"It's called being a celebrity." Crawford had warned her long ago about the perils of success. But she wasn't thinking of that now or of the approving truck driver or even of Crawford. She was thinking of Luke and his unfair questions.

"How do you feel, Ms Hale," he'd asked early in the show, "about being a traitor to the women's movement?"

As if she was! As if she needed to defend herself to the presumptuous host of a talk show. Actually, Jessica admitted to herself, she *would* have defended herself if she'd had a chance. Luke Maxwell never gave her that chance. But it wasn't just the personal attack that she resented; it was his presentation of her as an intelligent but shallow woman running an operation that Maxwell characterized as "pandering to the tastes of the overindulged and understimulated."

No, she wasn't going to let remarks like that go unchallenged.

Jessica swung out of the traffic and onto a side street, picked up speed and headed toward her office. An unaccustomed glint of revenge shone in her eyes as a favorite phrase of Crawford's popped into her mind. "Don't get mad; just get even."

She pulled into her private parking space behind the glass-and-steel tower that was the Modern Times' headquarters, turned off the ignition but didn't get out of the car. She was thinking about Luke Maxwell, and she wanted to shed the image that was trying to creep into her mind and shed it once and for all before going in to work. It was the image of his deep brown eyes that had a sparkle of mischievousness in them, the ingratiating smile that was also a little sexy, the sleepy bedroom voice tinted with cruelty—all the paradoxical parts of the man who'd seemed for a moment to believe her and then led his audience in an attack. It was that attack she wanted to remember; the rest she forced herself to forget: the walk, athletic and woodsy; the long lean body and the faint, just-barely-there hint of his after-shave. Those were the memories she shed as she sat back in the car's rich leather seat, and she shed them thoroughly. The richness of the car helped.

She'd bought it as a present for herself on the anniversary of her first year's survival at Modern Times. It had been a survival with style, and she was entitled to some mistakes along the way. "Speak Out" was a major mistake, but she planned to rectify that. Retaining the memory of Luke Maxwell, attacker, she opened the car door. She'd wasted too much energy in anger over him. She needed to turn that energy into something constructive by putting Luke in his place. By the time she stepped out of the low-slung car, planting her high-heeled sandals firmly on the pavement, she'd begun to formulate a plan.

Jessica had all the power of Modern Times Enterprises behind her—including three magazines with large staffs and unlimited resources. With that power she should be able easily to turn the tables on Luke Maxwell. Jessica slammed the door resolutely behind her and started across the parking lot. The decision was made: she'd find his weak spot. There had to be something in his life he didn't want revealed, something that wouldn't stand up under intense scrutiny. Business. . .personal. Jessica didn't care. She was going to play by his rules.

She hadn't been around for Maxwell's meteoric rise to fame. Those years had been spent traveling extensively for Modern Times, and when she had been in town it wasn't to watch television talk shows, even the most controversial and popular one. Surprisingly, their paths had never crossed. Less surprising was the fact that she didn't know anything about him. Few did. Those in the television medium who analyzed the news held a privileged position. Somehow they were always put on pedestals above the public domain. They were expected to delve but never to reveal themselves. Jessica had never figured out how that unspoken bargain evolved; she only knew it existed. There was an element in the media that was above reproach. Luke Maxwell would seem to belong to that element, if for no other reason than his association with the respected broadcasting giant, Arch Wheeler. Well, it was time one of those TV darlings had his halo examined, Jessica thought. She would start the ball rolling with Luke Maxwell.

She crossed the marble lobby with a breezy elegance and a sure determination. She knew exactly what to do. With the help of MT she'd turn this morning's debacle into a triumph for herself and the company. For the first time that day a genuine smile lit up Jessica's face. As usual, it was a smile that turned heads as she strode into her private elevator for the twenty-second ride to the penthouse.

Then she moved quickly, avoiding staff members who attempted to ask about her appearance on "Speak Out," which wouldn't be broadcast locally until five-thirty. "Don't rush home to see it" was Jessica's laughing comment just before she sought refuge in her office.

The room always had the power to soothe her. When she'd moved into the executive suite, Jessica had tossed out decorator ideas for both the popular high-tech look and the more feminine antique decor, and had opted instead for simplicity: pale oak furniture, desks and tables with large working surfaces, wonderfully restful colors—the blues, browns and beiges that pleased the eye and relaxed the mind. The whole ambiance was one of easy efficiency in which the setting didn't overpower the star. And at MT, Jessica was the star despite the efforts of some of the old guard to unseat her.

She dropped her briefcase next to her desk, sat down with welcome relief and with equal relief began to sift through the stack of telephone messages. These were problems she could handle.

But not yet. First things first, and the sooner Luke Maxwell was off her mind, the sooner Jessica could deal with the business at hand. She took off the jacket of her silk dress, tossed it over a chair and reached for the phone.

Ten minutes later the editor of *Scope*—one of MT's three magazines—was in her office. *Scope* specialized in the local scene, featuring slick and incisive personality pieces. The bright young staff was headed by Monty LaBaux, a slim dark French Creole with soft-spoken charm. He had the Frenchman's carefree nature and, in keeping with tradition, an eye for the girls.

Monty sank into the comfortable chair opposite Jessica's desk and threw her a look that suggested he was about to propose a brief dalliance over lunch. It wouldn't be the first time. He'd made the proposition before, at much less appropriate moments. He raised one eyebrow. Jessica waited. Then he posed his question.

"What can I do for you, boss?"

"Get that lascivious look off your face, first of all," Jessica ordered in a playful voice. This kind of banter often preceded their working meetings but had never gone beyond talk. Monty had told her his intentions over their first long dinner, and Jessica had firmly declined to be added to his long list of conquests.

"Suppose I narrow the list down to three or four?" he had asked.

"Even if you narrow it to one, you're not my type, Monty."

"What is your type?" He'd posed the question seriously on a few occasions, but Jessica had never been able to answer to the satisfaction of either Monty or herself, and she couldn't today, either. Once or twice Jessica had come close to falling in love, but something had been missing. Sometimes she wondered if she'd ever have the answer to Monty's question.

The look remained on Monty's face. "Can't help it, Jessica," he said as he leaned back in his chair, boldly eyeing his boss. "You're particularly beautiful today. A certain flush to the cheeks, a glow to the eyes. Could it be leftover excitement from your appearance on 'Speak Out'?"

"Something like that," Jessica equivocated. "You might even call it anger."

Monty gave her a quizzical look.

"He went for the jugular, Monty."

"Exactly what did you expect?" he responded pointedly.

"Somehow, that we'd discuss my professional life, the changes at MT, the new directions. It was rough; apparently he thought I could take it."

Monty shifted in the chair, crossed his legs, placing his right highly polished shoe on the edge of his left knee, and readjusted the pleat in his lightweight gabardine pants. Each movement was made with a deliberate kind of nonchalance, but his mind was really on Jessica. "And were you able to take it?" he asked.

"I think so, but I'm not sure the viewers will agree. Watch tonight and see for yourself."

"You probably came off better than you think," Monty reassured her.

"Perhaps, but I still object to his technique."

Monty looked across the desk and regarded his boss carefully without letting her good looks confuse the issue, which was possible for him, though not easy. He tried, not quite successfully, to dismiss his first impression that the glow on her face was excitement—not anger—over Luke Maxwell.

"Just what do you want me to do?" he asked carefully. Something was up.

"First, tell me about Luke Maxwell. All I know is that he's supposedly the wunderkind of Arch Wheeler's television station. What else?"

A knowing gleam danced in Monty's eyes. Give him a name in the news and he could break it down like a computer into all the relevant parts; dissect, analyze and interpret it. He was programmed with facts about every person and place of importance in the world. He missed nothing. That's why Jessica had hired him to edit *Scope* just after she took the reins at MT. That had been her first difficult decision, because many of the old guard hadn't been pleased to see the bright young Creole move into a place of importance, and they let it be known. But move Monty did, immediately setting fires under his editors and leaving them to put out the flames. Those who managed, stayed; those who faltered were soon gone.

Monty had really been after the editor-in-chief's job at *Modern Times* magazine. That's where the action was with Jessica initiating changes the whole country talked about in a magazine that was number five in subscriptions worldwide. But Crawford had chosen to keep the title—if not its responsibilities—for himself. It was his baby even though Jessica made most of the decisions. Except for the centerfold. That remained—Crawford had joined the old guard in that fight. It was left to Monty to keep making waves at *Scope* and bring the magazine out of the local market into prominence throughout the Southeast.

Monty considered the question about Luke Maxwell. Then he pushed a mental button and began to spout answers. His words spilled out at breakneck speed but quietly, efficiently. He knew his subject.

"Luke Maxwell first came to New Orleans as a professor at Tulane University. He's from the North, about thirty-five years old, self-made-man type, went to grad school in Massachusetts. His field is cultural anthropology. He has a Ph.D. but never uses the title Doctor; he's much too proletarian for that. Wheeler met him at a lecture series and was bowled over by Maxwell's philosophy, intelligence, charisma... whatever. Hired him about two years ago to develop and host 'Speak Out.' Seems the old boy didn't want a media type but someone with 'substance.' And Wheeler's foxy old intuition was right. 'Speak Out' became a hit and Maxwell the darling of America."

Jessica sat silent at her desk, soaking up Monty's words like a sponge.

"From what I hear," Monty went on, "Wheeler thinks Luke is cut in his own image—honest, incorruptible, a man of the people." He laughed at his own phrasing. "Sounds supercilious but appears to be true."

Jessica ignored that and asked, "Are you sure he's incorruptible?"

Monty shrugged. "I suppose everybody has a price, but I've never picked up any hint of dirty doings. And he takes them all on, the tough and the tender: politicians, journalists, revolutionaries, economists, the right and the left. . .and now a very beautiful corporation head."

Jessica didn't acknowledge that comment; instead she toyed with a pencil, doodling on a desk pad. "He intrigues me, this self-righteous Luke Maxwell."

Monty didn't seem surprised by that remark.

"Wouldn't it be interesting," she continued, "if the tables were turned?"

Monty nodded. He'd already figured out where she was going with her questions.

"He attacks his guests' vulnerabilities—either directly or with calculating charm. But what about him? There must be some vulnerability he doesn't want exposed." As she spoke Jessica's pencil traced the letters *LM, LM, LM* over and over.

"You're not the kind for vendettas, Jessica," Monty said as he tried to read something in Jessica's face and failed. "Apart from that, I like the idea. Those guys who ask the questions rarely have anything to answer themselves. That's just not democratic," he said with a smile, "and maybe *Scope* can lead the way, starting with a tough exposé of Luke Maxwell."

"I want to know everything about him," Jessica said quietly. "Every intimate detail of his life." Jessica's blue eyes met Monty's boldly and he dismissed his earlier supposition. This lady was out for blood.

"I'll send someone out to poke around," he agreed. "But remember, there's nothing derogatory to go on—no hidden mistresses or girlfriends of dubious character or vengeful ex-wives. If there were, I'd know."

Jessica laughed. "Even you don't know everything, Monty."

"I've got the facts. This guy's squeaky clean."

Jessica shook her head. "No one is perfect. You'll find something."

The assignment having been made, Monty got to his feet. "It goes without saying that we'll keep this quiet until we find your—something. Anybody special you want assigned?"

Jessica ran through a list of names in her mind before deciding. "Sharon Jessup, I think. Her article on our late great indicted district attorney was Pulitzer Prize material."

Monty, almost at the door, stopped, turned and flashed a wide smile that revealed perfect teeth. "You're not worried that she'll be subverted by Luke Maxwell's charms?"

"Would you ask that about a male reporter?" Jessica shot back.

"Touché," Monty answered as he reached the

door. In spite of his playboy image, Monty had a high regard for women and no resentment about working for one of the top women in corporate America.

"She directs, but never stifles, and she has imagination, which most men in high places lack," Monty often said of his boss, and others who worked below her at MT had begun, grudgingly, to agree with him. Today her imagination was going a little wild, Monty thought as Jessica made one final request before he disappeared out the door.

"I'd like to see the research and rough draft on this one before it's edited, Monty. Do you mind?"

He hesitated. As head of MT, Jessica could exercise editorial control although she'd never chosen to do so. Until now. It wasn't the usual procedure, but this wasn't the usual story. He decided to go along with her request. It might prove to be interesting.

When Monty left, Jessica began to relax. Luke Maxwell belonged to *Scope* now, and somewhere, somehow, *Scope* would take care of him through the auspices of the bright dependable Sharon Jessup. Jessica leaned back in her chair. The Luke Maxwell problem was over, or at least transferred elsewhere. There was nothing left of him here but the initials scribbled all over her note pad. With exaggerated resolution, Jessica tore off the page and tossed it into the wastebasket. It was the gesture she needed to put him from her mind completely.

At six-thirty Jessica's secretary came to the door, a scowl on her ebony face. Jessica looked up and almost laughed. No one had as much difficulty frowning as Toni.

"This is the fourth day in a row you've worked after quitting time. Don't you ever go home?" Toni tried to scold.

Jessica stretched tired arms above her head and leaned back against the now thoroughly wrinkled jacket she'd never bothered to hang up. "Occasionally," she answered, "but there's been a lot of work today."

"Too much, obviously. Judging from the cold tube over there—" Toni gestured to the TV in the wall console "—you didn't even watch your appearance on 'Speak Out.'"

"Hmm," Jessica responded prudently. "No time." She'd studiously avoided going near the television set for the past hour.

Toni, able to read her boss well, decided not to pursue the subject. "I guess we'll get into that later," she said with mock timidity.

"Probably not," Jessica shot back before smiling fondly at her secretary. She'd promoted Toni Allen from the typing pool and had been rewarded with an assistant who was intelligent, capable and always "up." She was a woman without a negative thought. She was also remarkably beautiful. The girl could have been a model, Jessica thought, glancing at the lanky black woman who leaned her five feet ten inches against the doorjamb with easy grace. Her makeup was startlingly bold, but it worked because Toni's face, crowned by close-cropped hair, was perfectly shaped and her features were unusual, particularly the huge eyes set wide apart. It was a face that called for something daring, and she was a woman who dared. She was also one who persisted, Jessica realized.

"Come on, Jessica," she prodded. "The day's over. Let's get out of here."

Jessica resisted. She still had an hour's work on her desk. "I'm not ready, but you take off. Aren't you late picking up Kadisha from the center?"

Jessica had opened day-care facilities on the ground floor to assist working mothers at Modern Times, and had found, to her delight and even surprise, that the facility paid for itself by decreasing the absentee rate. Three-year-old Kadisha had been the first child to walk through its doors, and she continued to be the star of the MT toddler set.

"Bobby picked her up for me. I've got school tonight," she reminded Jessica.

Jessica marveled that Toni could juggle work, a husband, a child, school "and still have time to put on my makeup," as Toni always responded when her list of accomplishments began to embarrass her.

"What's tonight?" Jessica asked. "Accounting?"

"Nope, marketing, and I need to get going." She still lingered, though, talking to Jessica, who had become more friend than employer. "Why don't you call that handsome guy you went out with last week, the one in real estate?"

Toni had a happy, if unusual, even somewhat chaotic, marriage, which she wished for everyone—especially Jessica. "Have him take you to dinner and leave all this behind."

Jessica shook her head. "No. I won't be seeing him again since I turned down his deal."

Toni opened her huge eyes wide.

"He wanted to sell me the property for our next corporate expansion—and I thought we had a date. It's what I call coming on strong!"

"Well, either that or they're overpowered by you," Toni said in defense of the unlamented salesman who'd been good-looking in a slick blond kind of way. "Now, how about the guy—"

"Toni, time for school." Suddenly Jessica didn't want to continue the conversation about her relationship with men. Most of them were too overwhelmed by Jessica's power and position at MT Enterprises to ask her out, and those who did usually had an angle—something they wanted from MT. Jessica had become very wary of exploitation.

But Toni had one more volley. "Now that Luke Maxwell's a foxy-looking guy. Real nice body. And he wasn't awed by you at all." Toni had made a point of watching "Speak Out."

"No, he certainly wasn't," Jessica agreed wryly.

Toni went a little further, testing. "It was a good show, Jessica, and you handled yourself well, considering. . . ."

Jessica waited.

"Well, considering they tried every dirty trick in the book. You'd think MT invented the H-bomb instead of the centerfold. But it was good publicity." Toni positioned her leggy body right in the middle of the doorframe. "And the way he looked at you—"

"Toni. . . ."

"Okay, okay. I'm leaving. Let the guard downstairs know if you decide to spend the night," she sang out over her shoulder as she strutted down the hall.

Jessica listened as Toni's footsteps faded, leaving her alone in the executive suite. All was quiet except for the hum of the air conditioning as it cut monotonously off and on. She was alone, but more than that, she was lonely. There was a difference.

Toni was right. She'd like nothing better than to call an old and good friend and go down to the French Quarter for dinner and a little jazz, but there were half a dozen memos to answer and no one she really wanted to call.

Except Crawford, and Jessica was afraid she'd become more dependent on him than she should be. He was a father to her and more; he was her whole family. The staff at corporate headquarters had become used to their relationship and their fierce loyalty to each other and understood it, but in the far-flung MT empire and beyond there were still comments that rankled Jessica and amused Crawford.

"Noblesse oblige," he'd told her. "Let them think what they will." Dillon, the ultimate southern gentleman, lived an aristocratic life at his plantation far removed from the mundane working world. Despite urgings from lawyers and bankers, he'd steadfastly refused to move the main office out of New Orleans. "What more perfect place for my enterprises," he often joked, "than 'the city that care forgot.'"

Jessica smiled to herself and reached for the phone to call him. Then she remembered that Crawford was on a cruise with friends off southern California. She could probably reach him ship-to-shore, but after some thought she dismissed the idea. He deserved time away from MT . . . and its president.

Jessica glanced at her watch, picked up a memo and forced herself to review the debits and credits of a foundering radio station the board was considering for possible purchase.

Jessica didn't stay the night, as Toni had predicted, but she was there until nine o'clock and back again at eight the next morning, greeted by a stack of newspapers on her desk—one of them featuring the photograph she'd set up. It captured perfectly the look of superiority on Jessica's face and Luke's expression of disbelief. But it was splashed across the front page, not of the local morning paper, but of the *Tattler*, one of the most notorious tabloids in the country.

"Damn," Jessica said aloud. She'd always been careful to avoid the *Tattler* staff and was surprised that she hadn't recognized the photographer. Evidently they'd scraped the bottom of the barrel and come up with an unfamiliar face, hoping for a break. Well, she'd given it to them.

"FEUD RAGES," the headline screamed dramatically. Since there'd been no reporter on the scene, there was no story, only a few lines blown way out of proportion by a determined copyreader on the night desk looking for some excitement. He'd also added an amazing caption underneath the photo: "War declared between the sexy young president of Modern Times and TV's charismatic host."

With a grimace, Jessica picked up the paper gingerly with two fingers, as if to avoid contamination, and dropped it into the wastebasket. That was the only way of dealing with the *Tattler*. Her staff were careful not to mention it, and in a few days everyone had forgotten, and finally—after traveling to district offices to put out fires in Los Angeles, Chicago and New York—so had Jessica.

It was a difficult two weeks during which she'd talked only briefly to Crawford on the phone to keep him advised of the problems that were popping up like mushrooms after a spring rain. Chicago, home office of advertising and sales for *Modern Times* magazine, was particularly worrisome. None of the staff was happy with the new focus of the magazine.

"We'll lose a lot of our old subscribers," she was told again and again.

"Let them go," Jessica replied daringly. "There'll be new ones." Each change had precipitated these arguments, which so far Jessica had survived. A graph of the sales over two years showed a rapid decline in subscriptions followed by a slow but steady increase. Current readership was approaching its highest level as Jessica held to her latest changes, confident that advertising would follow suit. However, she didn't bring up the centerfold. She wasn't that confident. Yet.

L.A. presented its own problems, and so did New York, and when Jessica finally returned home she was travel weary but pleased. She'd made progress in maintaining the managerial style she'd established at the beginning. It was working. But Jessica was tired, her desk was weighted down with work and her calendar filled with appointments. She glanced at the day's schedule and buzzed Toni immediately.

"Absolutely not!" Jessica said when her secretary appeared at the door. "I don't have time for endless inedible lunches, especially those followed by long-winded speakers."

"But you have to go," Toni declared. "Not everyone is invited to join the St. Charles Club, and you'll be introduced to the membership today. It's an honor—not to mention good for the image." Toni made it a point to be up on every business-related organization in the city. "And it'll be fun," she added with an optimism only Toni could muster.

"No." Jessica was adamant, forcing Toni to play her trump card.

"Mr. Dillon wants you to go." She smiled triumphantly. "He called and left this message." Bracelets jangled on her slim black arm as Toni dropped the phone slip on Jessica's desk.

Jessica read the message: *It never hurts to sup with the patricians. Be a good girl and go.*

"Outnumbered again," Jessica said with a laugh. "I can't fight both of you."

"You never could," Toni agreed with a dazzling smile as she assured Jessica that the menu wouldn't include Chicken Divan.

It didn't. The St. Charles Club, the oldest and most firmly established of the New Orleans business associations, met at the landmark Pontchartrain Hotel, in the Garden District. Jessica arrived a little late, just as lunch was being served, and slipped into her place at one end of the head table. She ate her way through the elaborate meal and chatted with the elderly gentleman next to her, who'd sponsored Jessica for membership. A well-known criminal lawyer and longtime friend of Crawford's, the attorney was no stranger to change, having been an advocate of women's rights and proud to sponsor a woman of Jessica's stature in this male-dominated group.

"High time, too," he declared. Jessica leaned forward to relay her thanks to the slightly deaf lawyer and glanced down the length of the head table.

There at the other end staring brazenly back at her was Luke Maxwell.

Jessica masked her surprise, nodded coldly in Luke's direction and swore silently as she speared a glazed carrot. He was wearing a name tag that indicated he, too, was among the honored today. Next time she'd check the guest list before accepting luncheon invitations, no matter what Toni—or Crawford—said.

She turned her attention back to the lawyer whose conversation, although a little loud, was fascinating, and decided to enjoy herself. The speaker, head of a large chain of department stores, was brief and witty. He turned to the business at hand, introducing the new faces in New Orleans business who'd been invited to join the SCC.

Jessica was the first. She stood to a round of applause and remained standing during the introduction, confident here among the movers and shakers as the vast and sprawling corporate structure of MT Enterprises was described in detail, including the changes and innovations she'd undertaken. The looks on the faces turned toward her had first admired her beauty and now admired her accomplishments, all of which she'd tried against all odds to describe on "Speak Out." As she sat down to another round of applause, she threw a triumphant smile in the direction of Luke Maxwell, but he was looking away, and her moment of glory dimmed.

Luke was the last to be introduced. "Fighter for truth and justice...the epitome of journalistic endeavor...." Jessica listened to the first few sentences of his introduction and then tuned out. Still, a wicked little smile curved her lips. After the *Scope* article, the approving city might look less kindly on its television darling.

The luncheon began to break up, with some members drifting into another meeting room for coffee and brandy. Jessica declined the invitation but stayed long enough to express her thanks to everyone. Crawford would ask about that, so she did it dutifully before slipping out a side door and starting toward her car.

On her heels was a man who'd been sitting in the back of the room at the press table. He moved into step with her as she hurried across the asphalt parking lot. Jessica recognized him. They hadn't dug down deep enough to find an unknown face this time: he was a reporter for the *Tattler*. Jessica chastised herself again for setting up the photo with Luke and beginning the ridiculous feud while she avoided the barrage of questions being thrown at her.

Joe Kennan was impossible to avoid, however. "Still looks like a feud to me, Miss Hale. Noticed you and Maxwell didn't speak today. Any comment on that?"

"Absolutely none," Jessica replied.

"I was watching your face when he was introduced. You sure didn't look pleased with what was said about him. In fact—"

Jessica turned to face the little man and looked him dead in the eyes. He smiled crookedly, a smile that distorted rather than lighted his face. His receding hairline gave his high forehead an endless look, aided by skin and hair that were the same shade of pale yellow. It was a face so ordinary that she remembered it. Joe Kennan was always around, and he was persistent.

"Look, Mr. Kennan," she said resolutely. "This is not an interview, and I'm not answering any questions. Except this: there's no feud." She turned on her heel once more, determined not to utter another syllable.

Jessica didn't realize that a second set of footsteps had mingled with the reporter's as he'd hastened after her. The deep male voice known by millions took her by surprise.

"Ms Hale is exactly right. There's no feud," he said. "Never was." Then he added with a grin, "Never will be. We have deep respect and admiration for each other." Luke's eyes danced as he moved closer and took Jessica's arm firmly in his hand. "In fact, Joe, Ms Hale and I are spending the afternoon together. So if you'll excuse us. . . ."

Luke started to move toward his car, but Jessica resisted. He looked down at her, waiting, as the reporter wrote frantically on his yellow note pad. If she refused to go with Luke, the scene would be ripe for another scandal. She knew it. So did Luke, and he smiled.

Mutely Jessica gave in to the inevitable and followed him to his car. Spending even five minutes with Luke Maxwell was the last thing on her agenda, but one look at the reporter who was still standing in the parking lot convinced Jessica to climb into the car. Temporarily defeated but still resolute, she slammed the door and turned her head to stare out the window so that she didn't have to acknowledge Luke's smile of triumph as he started the car.

3

"YOU'VE MADE YOUR POINT, Mr. Maxwell," Jessica said three silent blocks later. "No one is following us so you can stop the car and let me out."

His answer, before she even finished the sentence, was to turn off St. Charles Avenue onto the crowded expressway. There was no getting out now. "We told Kennan we were spending the day together, remember? I'd sure hate to disappoint him," Luke teased.

Jessica ignored the joke and reminded Luke, "*You* made that statement. All I said to the man was 'no comment.'"

"Usually wise, but now it's time to take action. I've considered our 'feud' from every angle and decided it doesn't have enough class for either of us."

"And you've also decided we should be friends?" she questioned, shaking her head disparagingly. "It's not that easy, Mr. Maxwell."

"Luke," he corrected. "Of course it is, if you just relax." He noted her silence and followed it with his own. This was going to take time, Luke realized; there was still anger left in her, and a little in him, too. "Remember," he said, "you're responsible for the *Tattler* pursuing us. You arranged for my very public put-down." His words were light but his voice wasn't. It was obvious that Luke Maxwell had been upset by the *Tattler* photographer. "I'm not used to having my picture splashed across its less-than-prize-winning pages."

"I wasn't exactly pleased myself," Jessica admitted ruefully. "However," she went on to defend herself, "it seemed like a good idea at the time—a sort of defense against your attack on me. After all, *you* started that." Jessica was perfectly aware that the conversation was deteriorating as they alternately placed blame, each anxious to have the last word. Well, she certainly hadn't had it on the show. Now was better than never.

Luke didn't take up the challenge again. A frown settled on his forehead as he switched his concern from the conversation to the traffic. Jockeying for a space, he changed lanes and headed for the bridge. Soon they were on the other side of the wide Mississippi. Then he glanced at her, and when he spoke his words were thoughtful. "After you stalked out of the studio so grandly—and elegantly—my ego was shattered. The damage only lasted a few days but my image of you has lasted ever since." And in case Jessica might think of that as a compliment, he qualified it. "I'm not used to being put down so thoroughly by a woman I've just asked to dinner."

Jessica looked out the window without comment. They'd left the expressway and were traveling up the west bank of the Mississippi.

"Your silence isn't helping, Jessica."

She turned back to him and spoke her feelings bluntly. "This outing and the conversation were both your ideas. If you're uncomfortable with either you can always take me back to the hotel and my car."

"Okay, okay. I've been warned. You're going to make it tough."

Jessica felt an immense sense of satisfaction. *Not tough enough,* she thought, but said nothing.

"You didn't like appearing on my show?"

Jessica looked at him, astonished. There was only one answer, which she pointedly refused to give.

"I'm sure it seemed like an ordeal at the time," Luke continued, unabashed, "but it actually turned out to be a very good show. I don't suppose you watched it?"

Jessica didn't bother to answer that, either; he hadn't expected her to.

"Do you ever watch 'Speak Out'?" he asked then, with something akin to hope in his voice.

"No," she answered simply.

He tensed, tried to cover his irritation, didn't quite succeed but managed to get back coolly to the point. "Then I should tell you that my guests are not usually—" he searched for the right term "—show-business personalities."

Jessica threw a hard look at him. "I'm not a 'personality,' either, Mr. Maxwell," she retorted, refusing to use his first name if only because he'd asked her to. "I'm president of Modern Times Enterprises, a multimillion-dollar corporation."

"But you have to admit that a certain aura of glamour—and yes, show business—surrounds you. Celebrity status just naturally accompanies that job."

"So be it," Jessica said, remembering Crawford's

very similar words. "It's up to the serious-minded to ignore that and face the issues, but you chose to go with the show biz-celebrity angle." Anger had crept back into her voice and she paused, carefully controlling it before she went on. "That's certainly your prerogative. Now could you please turn around and head back to town? I have a very busy schedule today."

Luke shook his head. "No. I'm determined to settle the problem between us. Once that's done, we'll go back."

"Until then?" she asked.

"I live just a couple of miles from here" was his answer. He didn't say anything else and neither did Jessica. As far as she was concerned, they would remain diametrically opposed; in the meantime, work was piling up at her office. But more disturbing than the work or the conflict was Luke himself. She'd succeeded in putting him from her mind—almost—and now she was sitting beside him in his car headed for his house. Toni would be pleased; Jessica was not.

She leaned back in stony silence before finally deciding to accept her fate and watch the spring go by. The countryside was green and fragrant with it. She could smell the lush season, feel it, even taste it in the air. It was the spring she'd noticed the day of the show and hadn't thought about since. It was very much with her now. A clump of daffodils along the roadside caught her eye and stayed with her until the next burst of flowers appeared. Any other time she would have enjoyed the drive; she almost enjoyed it now, but she caught herself. It would not be wise to relax, something told Jessica.

Luke slowed down and turned onto a narrow road that wound around an enormous oak tree before straightening out and heading like an arrow into the deep woods, guarded by the oak trees that lined their way, protective and a little frightening. The road widened slightly, and Jessica prepared herself for the white-columned mansion she expected to see looming just ahead, but Luke's house wasn't a mansion at all. It was a simple Louisiana-style raised cottage with a veranda hugging three sides.

They climbed the steps to the porch in silence; Jessica's surprised, Luke's slightly amused. "I used to have a place in the Quarter," he explained. "Life in the fast lane and all that. Then I found this, and I knew it was what I'd been waiting for." He opened the door and Jessica stepped into his house.

She liked what she saw—simple, modern, comfortable. Good taste was obvious here; so was money. They crossed the hall and walked into a living room on a Swedish rug woven with patterns of cream and wine. "Please sit down," Luke said, and Jessica obeyed, sinking into the comfortable brightly hued sofa and wondering who had supplied the good taste: Luke, a decorator—or a girlfriend.

Luke stood over her, looking down with that sexy half smile she remembered as being tinged with irony. She saw none of that now. It was an open smile followed by the offer of a glass of brandy. "Which we missed at the luncheon because of your fast departure. And our clever getaway," he added.

Jessica declined the drink. "I really need to get back

to town, so if we could go ahead and discuss—what was it you wanted to discuss, Mr. Maxwell?"

"That you call me Luke," he reminded her.

"All right, Luke. Now if that's all—" She reached for her handbag and started to get up, but he had already placed a gently restraining hand on her shoulder.

"No, that's not all. I ran the tape before the show was broadcast and edited it—somewhat," he said almost sheepishly. He paused, waiting for that to sink in, but when Jessica didn't respond he tried again. "I realized I'd been a little rough on you."

She raised her eyes to meet his. "You had to run the tape to see that?"

"Yes, actually I did. Sometimes during a show I miss those . . . details."

Jessica bristled but remained silent.

"So then I tried to correct my mistake." Jessica could tell the admission was difficult for him. "You weren't what I expected. . . ." His voice trailed off. Then he took a deep breath and added another admission. "Sometimes when I'm not on top of an issue, I react aggressively. You got a large dose of that."

Jessica still didn't respond. She glanced around the room instead, taking in the floor-to-ceiling bookcases and wondering briefly what she'd find there. Books could reveal a lot about character; however, Jessica felt pretty sure of this man's character without looking in his library. *Aggressive* was his own word. Yet the apology surprised her, and the admission of his shortcomings was barely less than astounding. Still, she wasn't about to let him off the hook.

"I really can't accept your blatant unprofessionalism as an excuse. No matter how apologetic you are now, I was made to look like a fool then—and in front of millions of people."

"You really should have a look at the tape, Jessica. It turned out to be a good show. My respect for you grew as it went on. That's very evident from about halfway, but by then it was too late. The audience was off and running. There's no way I can control their questions. After all, my job is to put on a good program. And it was good."

"You chose the woman in the pink pantsuit on purpose." Jessica threw in the complaint that still rankled her.

"Wrong. If you'd been doing this job as long as I have, you'd know that the least likely people come up with the best questions. What I was hoping for was a bit of levity; I didn't expect ignorance. That was one of the sections I edited out."

"Hmm," Jessica managed, unbelieving.

Luke noted her doubt. "You're not an easy woman, Jessica Hale."

"I'm not in an easy business, and I don't like to be humiliated in public any more than you do."

"And you think you've been humiliated?"

"Yes."

"Well, I have been, too, by that front-page spread in the *Tattler*. So let's call it even." He moved to sit beside her on the sofa—not close, but close enough to make her uncomfortable. They sat side by side, Luke thoughtfully quiet, Jessica stiff and tense. He broke the strained silence. "Just listen to me, Jessica, as one professional to another. Don't you often print tough, no-holds-barred interviews in your magazines?"

"Yes, but—"

"Hear me out. My job is to ask questions—sometimes hard ones, questions my guests would rather avoid. My integrity, which you so haughtily challenged, depends on asking those questions. Just because I found you bright and sexy and fascinating didn't mean I'd turn the interview into a puff piece. I asked nothing of you that hadn't been asked before," he said defensively.

"And that's the point," Jessica snapped. "I expected some intelligent new questions, not a rehash of the past."

"But as a newsman I can't ignore the past, can I? Pretend it never happened? You know that."

She was silent. What he said was true. Background material was a mainstay of most news stories.

Grudgingly she nodded. "Maybe I overreacted to the question about the centerfold. It's one of the changes I haven't been able to make," she admitted.

"I'm like that too," Luke said conversationally. "Always more concerned with the things I haven't achieved than the ones I have."

Jessica shot a quick and wary look at him. He was good, really good. Already he'd made them equals, two pros fighting the same fight. She looked away, hardening her voice and her resolve. "I came on your program in good faith hoping to discuss some of the changes taking place at MT; instead, you set me up as a traitor to women, which just isn't true."

"Prove it," he said suddenly. "Come back on the

show. I'll do my homework this time. I'll be ready, and so will you."

Jessica looked at the man beside her. Handsome, impeccably dressed in a three-piece suit, intelligent—and very apologetic—he was still her nemesis, and she wondered what the hell he was up to.

Whatever it was, Jessica wasn't interested. "I'll never go on 'Speak Out' again," she said emphatically.

Luke shrugged his shoulders. "I guess you're right. If you came back on, I might really embarrass you. I'd read up on everything about MT, learn all the peripheral facts. I'm very good at that. Have a photographic memory, actually. . . ." He smiled modestly. "I'd probably murder you."

"I'm not taking the bait, Luke," she warned him.

Luke chuckled. It was obvious in his eyes when he looked at Jessica that he liked her. She was an easy woman to talk to, even when she was being tough. She was beautiful and bright and witty. "In another time, we could have been great friends. Even lovers," he added in a low voice that hinted at intimacy. "Unfortunately, I'm Luke Maxwell, upstanding talk-show host, and you're Jessica Hale, head of the naughty Modern Times."

Jessica laughed. "I've been called a lot of things, but never naughty. That's so Victorian, Luke."

"Didn't you know I'm very old-fashioned?"

She laughed again and he joined her, and that mingled sound penetrated the armor they'd both put on against each other's barbs.

"Can this mean I'm forgiven?"

Jessica nodded. "I may forgive but I won't forget," she warned. She didn't want this to get any more friendly, certainly not any more intimate. He was still sitting beside her with his arm around the back of the sofa, but he was much closer than before. She moved slightly and then reminded him, "Now that everything's settled, I really do need to get back to work. I have an afternoon filled with appointments."

"You can cancel them from here."

"No, Luke, really, I—"

"Please, Jessica, listen to me. I said earlier that we'd go back when this thing was settled between us. It's not settled yet."

"Meaning it will be?"

"If you'd give me a chance. I know you're fair. I've found that's a typical trait among the heads of mega-corporations. Fairness, honesty . . . ."

He was fishing again, but Jessica had to smile at his bravado—and his determination. She liked that in a person. Yet she was trying very hard not to like Luke Maxwell.

He'd seen the quiver of a smile that played on her lips, and he took advantage of her lapse. "We've negotiated a shaky truce. I'd like to cement it. Half-way through the show, I was charmed by you. At the end of it, I was hooked. God, you were good—even with the audience against you. When I asked you to dinner, I meant it. I wanted to see you again. I'll admit the photograph put a damper on my feelings for a while—but not for long. The luncheon brought everything back. You looked spectacular today." He let his hand drop until his fingers barely touched her hair. "That's why I decided to kidnap you. Thanks to Joe Kennan, it was easy; otherwise, I'd probably have thrown you over my shoulder."

Jessica was becoming tense again, with his fingers still lingering on her hair. He noticed her stiffen and moved his hand away. "Now that you're here," he continued, "I don't want to let you go, not for a couple of hours, anyway. Call your office," he pleaded. "Tell them you've been tied up."

"Kidnapped and held captive," she remarked. "You have the car keys, Luke."

"I knew you'd see it my way," he said with a smile. "Now, let's have that brandy. Then I want to show you around." He got up and headed for the bar to fix their drinks. Jessica's voice caught him in midstride.

"I didn't say I was staying," she reminded him. "I can very easily call and have a car sent. After all, power does have certain privileges."

He turned to look at her. "Power also has responsibilities: to learn the truth and to see both sides. Spend some time with me, Jessica. Learn what I'm really like." He was very appealing now, using all the weapons in his arsenal of persuasion. "Just give me an hour or so to show you around. I guarantee you'll find the afternoon worthwhile. If not, well, you can chalk it up to experience and write me off. But give me a chance," he asked again.

She glanced at her watch. The afternoon was almost gone. By the time she got back to her car and fought the traffic to her office, her staff would have left. "All right," she agreed. "I'll take the afternoon off, but," she cautioned, "I have to be back in New Orleans for dinner."

"No problem," Luke answered.

A smile curved Jessica's lips as she watched him pour the brandies. He wasn't as smart as he thought, inviting the enemy into his private domain. And she was still the enemy—as long as he wasn't sitting too close. She'd have to be careful about that. Meanwhile, she'd enjoy his hospitality while her staff dug up the goods on him. The irony of that appealed to Jessica.

Luke looked pleased with himself when he handed her the drink. Something in his smile, in his body language, told Jessica he was an easy man to read. She was pleased, too, as she accepted the drink with a smile. The reasons for their pleased looks were not the same.

Jessica saw in his eyes at least a hint of what Luke was thinking, that she was a beautiful woman with a good mind. He was interested. Definitely interested. She'd seen that look during the show—and more boldly afterward when he asked her for dinner. Because he'd been able to handle her so easily on "Speak Out," he might just be planning another conquest here in his house. If so, he was in for one hell of a surprise.

That was what Jessica was thinking. She was also thinking revenge, but he was sitting close to her again, and she reminded herself to be careful.

The room where they sat was very homey and informal, much like a den. She suspected the whole house had a warmth about it, and that warmth was her second surprise. The man she'd gotten to know—and be wary of—in the two encounters so far, didn't belong in this setting. It was disconcerting to see him here, confusing. More so when he began to talk about his house, his farm, life here away from the high wire.

"I'd really like to show you around," he said finally, putting down his empty glass. "Why don't you make that call to your office now and then take a ride with me, Jessica? The phone's on the desk." Without waiting for an answer, Luke disappeared out the door and down the hall. "I'll be right back," he called out.

Jessica obediently picked up the phone, dialed her office and told a bewildered Toni to cancel all afternoon appointments. "Just tell everyone I was called out of town. I'll explain tomorrow."

When Luke didn't return right away, Jessica decided to have a look at his books. As expected, many of them were written by guests on his show. She pulled out a fat biography and found, also not unexpectedly, that it was signed in glowing terms. The writer had, no doubt, escaped crucifixion on "Speak Out." There were, of course, texts on anthropology, books by pioneers in the field—Benedict, Malinowski, Mead. But the newer experts were represented, too. Jessica's fingers rested lightly on the books; this was a side of Luke she'd almost forgotten. Professor Maxwell.

The bookshelves literally turned the corner and continued into the hall, and Jessica wandered out with them. She passed a room with the door ajar. It was a den, small and dark and very appealing, a quiet room complete with an elaborate stereo system. In one corner was a guitar. She couldn't imagine the host of "Speak Out" strumming on that instrument and surmised that it probably belonged to a friend. Continuing down the hall, she almost ran into Luke as he came out of the bedroom.

"Exploring, I see," he commented with a smile.

"I just followed your library into the hall," Jessica explained. She didn't mention her pause at the door of the den.

"The books keep proliferating," Luke said. "Sometimes I feel like the Disney character who forgot the word to stop the deluge."

Jessica tried to concentrate on the books, feigning something that approached interest, but she wasn't interested anymore. She couldn't stop looking at Luke, who had surprised her again. He'd changed clothes and was wearing faded jeans that hugged his lean hips and muscular thighs. His plaid cotton shirt was open halfway down the front exposing his broad chest matted with dark hair. The shirt-sleeves were rolled up over lightly tanned forearms rippling with sinewy muscles. She could only think that he was too well built for an anthropologist—or a talk-show host. Before she could comment on his change of attire, Luke shoved a shirt and jeans into her arms.

"You can change in there," he said, nodding toward the bedroom. "It's tour time."

Jessica looked at the clothes she was suddenly holding and then up at him.

"I keep a few things in every size," he teased, and

when she nodded knowingly, he attempted an honest explanation. "Actually these belong to someone from the past. She lives in Baton Rouge now—"

Jessica held up her hand to stop him. "No explanations necessary. I'm not at all interested in the intimate details of your life," she lied.

"That's good because I blush whenever I have to reveal them," he joked back at her.

Jessica felt adequately put in her place as she followed his nod and went to change. Obviously, he had no intention of supplying details for her, and there didn't seem to be any revealing ones in his bedroom. She pulled on the jeans as she looked around. The four-poster bed was queen-size and extra long—but Luke Maxwell was a big man. There was an antique oak desk in the corner and a small table by the window, which looked out onto a wooded backyard.

The jeans were too long. Jessica rolled them up, slipped on the shirt and returned her attention to the breakfast table, large enough to accommodate two, but used most recently as a desk. There was a woman's touch—a bud vase at one end of the table, but it was empty and a little dusty. There'd been no romantic breakfasts here for a while, she thought as she buttoned the shirt—or tried to. It was a bit tight across her breasts, snugly molding to the contours of her figure.

Another quick look around the bedroom revealed nothing. This was simply a pleasant room in a warm livable house. An unused bud vase and some good books didn't add up to much of a past. Even the clothes she was wearing revealed only that he'd had a girlfriend, one who hadn't been around lately.

Jessica cast a glance in the mirror and hoped Sharon Jessup was having more luck. The only naughty thing in this house was the way Jessica looked in the borrowed blouse. Carrying her high heels, she walked back down the hall to the living room where Luke was waiting for her.

"You're certainly not very tall, Jessica," he commented as he stared down at her.

"I make up for lack of stature by sheer determination." Without her heels, Jessica barely came to his shoulder. He seemed even taller than in the studio, bigger than life. Instinctively she stepped away from his masculine presence and held up her shoes. "These didn't go with the rest of the outfit," she said. "I suppose the tour will have to be cancelled." Because she still hesitated to spend the afternoon alone with Luke, Jessica's remarks were half-serious.

Not to be deterred, Luke located a pair of woman's tennis shoes in a back closet and watched her intently as she put them on. "I hope they fit better than the blouse," he said as Jessica tried to ignore his sparkling eyes and tie the shoelaces. "It's a little tight, isn't it?"

"I hadn't noticed," she said airily. "But if it doesn't bother you, it doesn't bother me."

"I can assure you I'm not bothered in the least." He held out his hand to pull her up. "Come on. I want to show you my world."

A narrow road veered away from the house and along a clover-covered field. They walked silently for a quarter mile through the soft scent of the clover.

Luke reached for her hand, but after a few moments, Jessica removed her fingers from his. She'd agreed to a tour of his place, nothing more. They passed a frame house from which an elderly but tough and wiry little man emerged, recognized Luke and laconically waved him on. In the distance was a barn. They headed for it.

"Another side to the unpredictable Luke Maxwell. Are there actually animals in the barn?" she asked.

"Not just animals. Perfect specimens of horseflesh unequalled anywhere," he boasted. "Just wait."

They entered the barn. It was cool and dark as they walked along the bed of mulched hay. Tiny insects flitted and darted in the rays of sunlight that filtered through the slats high above the loft. A soft whinny came from one of the stalls, and Luke whispered to her. "That's Thetis," he said almost reverently as a velvety golden nose poked over the stall door. "Thetis and Hector," Luke explained. A second golden head appeared from the next stall, looking a little less friendly.

Luke led the palomino mare out into the filtered sunlight where she gleamed like golden cream. He gently tapped one hock and the mare stretched into a perfect show pose, her head high for Jessica to admire as a faint breeze ruffled her silvery mane and tail.

"She's a beauty," Jessica murmured, and Thetis seemed to shake her head in agreement.

Luke released his hold. "Take her out," he said to Jessica. Then he stepped back and watched, leaving her holding onto the mare's halter.

Jessica reached for a lead rope, hooked onto the

halter, and with one hand next to the horse's head, the other trailing the rope, led her out of the barn. Luke shook his head approvingly. He should have known. He followed behind with Hector. The gelding was a hand higher and wider across the chest and no less handsome than the mare.

"I had no idea. . . ." Jessica said as they emerged into the sunlight.

"That I was a lover of horseflesh?" Luke stroked Hector's shining neck. "I'm still surprised myself. When I bought this place I got a few extras like the barn and the tenant house, including Sam and his wife! Old Sam talked me into these two. He neglected to mention what they'd cost me in upkeep, but it's been worth every penny."

"They're magnificent," Jessica said.

"I'm glad you agree. Let's saddle up and ride. You do ride, don't you?" he asked, knowing the answer.

"Of course. I went to school in Virginia."

"English saddle, then, I suppose."

She nodded and a smile of approval danced in his dark eyes. Luke rode western saddle. He was a city boy, he told her, born and reared in South Boston. Country life was new to him. "But I'm learning," he said as they tied up the horses and brought out the tack from the barn.

Luke slung the saddles over the fence and they began to curry the horses. "I'm trying to learn all the ins and outs," he told Jessica. "I'm still a little wary of walking behind this big animal."

"Just grab his tail first, so he'll know where you are," Jessica said, demonstrating.

"I'll try that—later," Luke responded with a grin.

They worked quietly side by side, and the familiar scents of leather and horseflesh and new-mown hay brought back vivid memories to Jessica of poignant early-morning rides through the rolling hills of Virginia. She'd loved horses then and been content to ride on and on, never ready to bring her mount into the stable at day's end. Yet she hadn't been on a horse in years. Somehow since she'd begun her climb in the business world, there hadn't been time. She was envious that Luke made the time in his busy schedule.

Once the horses were saddled, Jessica mounted Thetis, and Luke swung up on Hector easily.

"Getting up is no problem," he admitted. "It's staying on that gives me trouble."

Jessica tried unsuccessfully to hide her grin. She was seeing a new side of Luke Maxwell, a side that—against her will—she found rather endearing.

They set off together for the river. Swollen with spring rains, muddy and brown and a mile wide, the Mississippi thundered past, rushing along its ancient path to the Gulf of Mexico. There was an abundant peace on its banks, and it was a peace Jessica hadn't felt in years. She rode along beside Luke and now and then their calves touched, causing her to turn the mare's head and put a few inches between them. He'd look at her quizzically when she moved away, but he wouldn't speak. They rode more than a mile that way, silent, bordered by the levee on one side and on the other by black fields just beginning to shoot forth the first green sprigs of spring. Above, the towering oaks guarded their unique peace.

The day had taken as many turns and twists as the river and its blossoming levee. Luke had virtually kidnapped her and then conned her into staying with him. The beautiful horses and the ride through the soft spring day had been a surprise that was more enjoyable for being so unexpected.

The farther they rode side by side through the woods with the sounds of the birds, the river and their own soft voices mingled together, the more relaxed she became, the more she could feel her guard slipping. Abruptly Luke reined in his horse and turned around on the path, beckoning Jessica to follow. He seemed to have made a decision, and she rode after him, curious.

Luke urged the big gelding into a gallop, and Jessica pursued him, bending low over the horse's withers to avoid low-hanging branches as they cut off the path onto another, more narrow, and came to a stop finally in a secluded clearing. Tucked beneath a sprawling tree at the edge of the clearing was a log cabin.

"The house that Luke built, literally," he said with a proud smile.

"You built it?" Her voice was incredulous. The day had held too many surprises.

"Well, Sam helped some," he admitted, "but I did most of the work myself." He hesitated, almost shyly. "Would you like to see it?"

"Would I!" They swung down from the horses, left them to graze in the clearing and headed for the cabin with Jessica still shaking her head in disbelief.

Inside was one large room with an unfinished loft

overhead. The walls were rough-hewn logs, the floor wide planks. There was very little furniture—a daybed in front of the fireplace, a pile of colorful pillows, a table with four chairs.

"Simple, eh?" Luke said. "But it has possibilities."

Trailing her hand along the rough wood walls and the cold fireplace stones, Jessica circled the room. There were ashes in the grate.

"On the rare occasions when I can get away, this is my retreat," he said, answering her unasked question. "It's still pretty primitive. No electricity. I build a fire, throw lots of blankets over me—" he laughed a little self-consciously "—and try to recapture the childhood I never had, I suppose." He leaned back against the table and watched as she continued her trip around the room and then up the ladder to peep into the loft.

"It'll be a sleeping loft when I get it finished. Next year, if I'm lucky. What we've done so far has taken two years, working on weekends when I can get away." Jessica looked over her shoulder at him from her position on the ladder. He seemed young and rather vulnerable and, like a boy, proud of his accomplishment.

"I made the table, too, and the chairs," he said with a crooked smile. His feet, clad in old leather cowboy boots, were crossed in front of him, and his hands were pushed down into the jeans pockets. Boyish, she thought again. Yet the way he looked at her told her this was no boy.

He moved quickly toward her, and before Jessica could clamber down from the ladder, he trapped her there, close enough for her to feel his breath against her hair, his chest against her back. The warmth emanating from his body was like a fire that left its hot imprint on the skin. She could have moved away from the fire, but she couldn't move away from Luke, so she stood silently, holding on to the ladder, waiting. . . .

Luke's arms slid around her waist. "I'm glad you like the cabin, Jessica. I knew you would. That's why I turned around and brought you back here. It was unplanned; I hadn't meant to come here today. This is a part of my life that I don't share often."

The surprises would never end, it seemed. Luke Maxwell, whom she'd started out to hate, had cared enough to bring her into his own special world. "At the luncheon I couldn't bear the sight of you," she said. "And now we're. . . we're. . . ." Jessica stumbled, searching for the right word.

"Friends, I hope," he said, his lips almost touching the shine of her hair. "Will you stay and have dinner with me? I have lots to offer. . . good wine, good conversation, good food, which I'll cook myself," he bribed.

She shook her head firmly. "Remember your promise to have me back in New Orleans in time for dinner?"

"Big date?" Now his mouth was touching her hair.

She hesitated. She could lie or tell the truth. She opted for the truth. "No plans; I just needed an out. This isn't a date, Luke. It's an afternoon of. . . of. . . ." Jessica realized she was stumbling, searching for words, and she knew why. He was standing too close to her, touching her with the lean length of his body.

"I'd like it to be a date," he said, "to make up for the dinner you turned down after my show. Admit it, Jessica, you've had fun today—the horses, the cabin. I think you've even enjoyed being with me. And after all," he added philosophically, "you have to eat somewhere." He waited expectantly.

Jessica leaned her forehead against a rung of the ladder. How could she argue with anything he'd said? He'd apologized more than adequately, given her his side of the "Speak Out" episode logically and persuasively and asked her back on the show for another try. She was beginning to believe he wasn't the cold calculating egomaniac she'd thought. In fact, she and Luke were a great deal alike: two ambitious determined people trying to do their jobs. She felt her resolve slipping away, tried to recover and then gave up.

"Okay," she agreed. "You're on."

Jessica felt him relax and then move back so she could step off the ladder. The physical contact was broken, yet the intimacy that had been created by the heat of his body next to hers lingered and bathed them in a glow as warm as the embers of a dwindling fire. They galloped the horses back to the barn, left them for Sam to unsaddle and rub down, and headed for the house, tired, hungry and this time hand in hand. The last rays of sunlight were just slipping behind the trees as they stepped inside.

True to his word, Luke cooked dinner—steaks broiled on a grill near the back door. Jessica made the salad, sitting on a stool beside the wide oak counter and chopping away as she talked to Luke about some of the issues she hadn't been able to bring up on "Speak Out." He listened quietly most of the time, argued a little and asked a lot of questions, which encouraged her to go on.

"I don't understand it," she said in an impassioned voice. "TV and newspapers are filled with violence and death and bloodshed, which we accept as a matter of course. *Modern Times* dares to talk realistically about the relationships between men and women, and we're vilified." Her cheeks were flushed and her eyes shone with righteous indignation. "Well?" she said to Luke who was leaning against the kitchen counter, hands in pockets, looking at her. "No response?"

He walked around the counter, took away the knife she'd been wielding so dramatically, removed the carrot from her other hand and proceeded to cut it up for the salad. "I have two comments. First, you should come back on the show. Second, you are an exceptionally intelligent and beautiful woman. Now, let's eat."

After dinner, Luke lit a fire and Jessica curled up on one end of the sofa, wineglass in her hand, gazing into the orange-blue flames.

Luke watched her for a long time before wondering aloud about her thoughts.

"Thinking about today," she admitted. "And you."

He reached for her hand. "What made you decide I wasn't a direct descendant of Attila the Hun?"

Jessica wished he would sit down beside her just as earlier she'd wished he'd move away. That's what a few hours had done to change her feelings about Luke Maxwell.

Then he did sit down, not beside her but on the other end of the large overstuffed sofa. "What made you change your mind, Jessica?" he asked again.

"An entire day of surprises," she answered softly. "This house, so unlike what I expected. Your apology—"

"Also not expected," he said for her.

"No. Not at all. Then there were those two horses. . . ."

"I knew it. She likes the animal lover in me." He lightened the moment with those words, but Jessica, he realized quickly, was very serious.

"The cabin did it. Well, not so much the cabin as your taking me there. That was the biggest surprise in a day full of surprises. You're not at all what I thought."

"You're everything I thought—and more." He reached across the expanse of sofa, took the wineglass from her hand and moved closer. "More charming." He lifted her hand to his lips and kissed each finger thoughtfully. "More human. Warmer." His lips moved to her wrist, bared for his kiss by her rolled up shirt-sleeve.

"I think I like all this praise," Jessica said. "Don't stop now."

"More opinionated." He turned her hand over and kissed the palm. His lips were warm, his breath, too, on her sensitive skin. "More stubborn."

"You can stop now," she said, meaning the description, not the rest.

"More beautiful," he said, kissing her cheek. "Sexier." His mouth found hers, and Jessica's lips opened to accept the kiss. She slipped her arms around his neck and gave herself to the first sweet taste of him, full of promise, ripe with hope.

The flames from the fire reflected in his glasses and set his smoky eyes ablaze. "Your glasses," she murmured between kisses. "Don't you ever take them off?"

"Only in bed," he whispered into her ear, and before the sentence was complete, she'd reached up and pulled them off. He took the glasses from her with a laugh and put them on the table and then tucked her comfortably in his arms.

She was ready to return his kisses, letting her lips touch his high cheekbones and his eyelids and his forehead—all those places that were available to her now. His face was her canvas, and she painted him with kisses. She could feel the quickening of his breath and the racing of his heart as he lay back against the pillows, holding her close and letting her lips work their magic.

"There's one more word for what you are," Luke said.

"What?" she asked, drawing back a little to look at him.

"Trouble. Devilish and imaginative trouble. Only women with something on their minds take off my glasses. I wonder—"

"What?" she asked, kissing him again.

"How far you're willing to go after that bold gesture."

Jessica didn't answer; she wasn't sure. He read the uncertainty in her eyes, and with hands that sought to change her mind, pulled her even closer, crushing her breasts against him as with an impatient mouth he devoured her, his tongue touching, caressing, tasting, soft velvet on softer satin.

His hands moved deliberately across her back, molding her against him like a supple reed. One hand strayed to her shoulder, moved along her collarbone and trailed downward. His touch was electric as he cupped her breast and rubbed his palm insinuatingly against her taut nipple, and it jolted them both. One of the buttons pulled open on her tight shirt, and at last his hand found the soft bare skin of her breast. He tore his lips from hers and buried his face in her hair with a low moan.

"For weeks I've dreamed of touching you there," he said, "and there." He moved his hand farther inside her shirt and caressed her nipple with his fingertips. "Jessica," he moaned, "I want you."

Again she couldn't answer. It was too soon. He drew away, removed his hand, and still holding her close, sat back on the sofa. "Jessica?" he asked softly.

She touched his face with her fingers, tracing the line of his forehead and cheek. "Everything's happened too fast, Luke. I don't want to make a foolish mistake. I need some time."

"I'll give you time, Jessica. All you want, if you'll just be straight with me. Is it really time you need . . . or is there someone else?"

Jessica laughed softly. "With my busy schedule?"

"Not even Crawford Dillon?" Luke tried to keep

his voice casual, but there was a suspicious edge to it that made her stiffen in his arms.

"You believe those stories?" Disappointment surged through her.

"No," he reassured her almost too quickly. "But I want you to tell me. This isn't for the public. Say it to me."

Gently she pushed a strand of hair from his forehead. "There's no one else, Luke." She reached over and picked up his glasses and slipped them back on. "That was a little presumptuous of me," she admitted.

"Just remember, next time it's for real. Until then it's just you and me, babe."

"What about 'Miss Baton Rouge'?" she asked slyly.

"I'll mail the clothes back tomorrow."

"And the shoes?"

He repeated the wry smile. "They weren't hers," he said and added quickly before she had a chance to even raise an eyebrow, "I'll mail them back to Shreveport first thing tomorrow."

Jessica smiled. She knew he would.

FORTUNE'S REST WAS BUILT in the 1850s when cotton was king and homes along the Mississippi were forty-room mansions. Crawford Dillon had bought it from the impoverished descendant of the original owners and spent a cool half million restoring it to its former glory. He lived there in style, as lord of the manor, usually ensconced in his rocking chair on the white-columned veranda looking out across the formal gardens to the river beyond.

In a way Jessica had grown up here. After her mother's death she and her father had been Crawford's frequent guests. Jessica's fondest memories were of long lazy Sunday afternoons sitting on the steps while the men talked business, politics and world affairs—with a little New Orleans gossip thrown in for good measure. She'd come to parties at Fortune's Rest as a child, dances as a teenager, and when her father died she'd come to Fortune's Rest to live.

Jessica was comfortable sitting here on the steps again, leaning against one of the broad white columns while Crawford rocked beside her nursing his mint julep. He was the last of a dying breed who still drank the concoction, served up in an initialed sterling silver Jefferson cup, the crushed mint from his herb garden, the bourbon from a special reserve. Preparation for the drink was a daily ritual whenever Crawford was in residence at Fortune's Rest.

Today, in the quiet of late afternoon, Jessica sipped a glass of white wine and relaxed while Crawford threw her questions. They hadn't seen each other for a while, and she'd driven out this weekend to go over the bulging folder of memos and reports that needed his attention. After working inside for a couple of hours, they'd moved to the veranda. The tough part was over; the easy camaraderie had begun.

Crawford leaned back in his chair and watched his protégée with loving eyes. She seemed different to him today, softer, more relaxed. A good time, he decided, to broach the next topic.

"Now, what about that show, Jess?" It was a probing question, softened by his southern drawl. That drawl—and his store of puns and adages—made Crawford seem like an easy man, a little slow and lazy. Jessica knew better and so did everyone who'd done business with Crawford Dillon. He was greatly respected and greatly feared. Even his wife and son had been in awe of his power. Only Jessica had been able to love him outright with no reserve and no hesitation. She appreciated the tough spirit that raged beneath the white linen suits and striped bow ties. She appreciated the probing mind and hard questions. Today, however, she could have done without them.

She sipped at her wine before answering. "I'd actually rather forget about that show."

"Don't blame you, honey," he drawled. "Maxwell was pretty tough on you."

"How do you know? You were supposed to be on a cruise."

"Taped it."

"Of course," she said. "You would have."

He rocked silently for a while and then asked, "What did you learn from your appearance on 'Speak Out'?"

Jessica's answer was emphatic. "Never go into an interview without being prepared—for the worst!"

Crawford threw back his head and laughed. It was an abundant laugh, which Jessica had always loved, a rumbling comfortable laugh that started low in his chest and then gradually exploded into guffaws. He was a man who loved to laugh. "Good maxim to live by, Jess. Next time you'll no doubt capture the audience just as you captured Luke Maxwell. . . ."

Jessica looked up in surprise, started to speak and then decided to wait for him to explain that one. It took a while.

Crawford rocked up in his chair, planted both feet firmly on the porch floor, put his drink beside the rocker and began to look serious. He was a grand-looking man with a hawklike face, a beak of a nose and dark intense eyes. It was not a pretty face but an appealing one. Women adored him, and Jessica knew he had an active social life, but he'd suffered great pain in losing the two people he loved most in the world, and Jessica knew he'd never marry again.

Crawford liked a little romance in his life, though, and he constantly worried that it was missing from

Jessica's. Men were wary of her, intimidated by her. Maxwell was neither of those.

Crawford picked up his glass again, drained it and called out for a refill. A servant materialized immediately with a frosty pitcher. Jessica declined more wine and waited for Crawford's next words. They were observant.

"Hell, you can't fool me. If he didn't make a pass at you that very day, he's gotten around to it since."

Jessica shook her head. "You are astounding, Crawford. I often wonder if it's intuition or good spies."

Crawford laughed again, heartily. "Sometimes both. This time nothing but good eyesight. I watched you two trying to avoid the attraction because of the antagonism, but it didn't work. There was so much electricity between you, I was surprised the TV didn't shatter."

"Toni saw it, too," Jessica admitted.

"'Course she did. The gal's no fool. So let's hear about it, Jess."

She launched into the story obediently, omitting nothing, from Luke's dinner invitation after the show to their day together at the river. Crawford took a long swig of his drink and stared out over the gardens, which were already profuse with spring. He usually spoke his mind without hesitation. She could only imagine that he didn't like Luke for some reason.

"You disapprove of him?" she asked warily.

"Hell no. Besides, I don't set myself up to judge. You know that. I was just thinking about the past and the effect it might have on the future. Your future."

"I really am puzzled now."

"I reckon you would be since I never told you anything about it. In fact, when it all happened, you weren't more than knee-high; I didn't even know your dad then. Years later, it didn't seem important enough to go into."

"What, Crawford, for Lord's sake?" Jessica was intrigued and a little uneasy. "Is it about Luke?"

"Yes and no. About his boss, Arch Wheeler. Arch and I go back a long way."

Nothing could have surprised Jessica more. The two men seemed to have little in common, and she'd never heard Crawford mention Arch Wheeler, even in passing. Yet now that she thought about it, they must have known each other, for they were both influential forces, probably the two most powerful men in New Orleans. It was inevitable that they had met. But Jessica was about to learn that there was much more.

By the thoughtful way he sipped his bourbon, she could tell this was going to be quite a story. And she was right. Over the course of that drink and another, she learned that more than twenty years earlier, Crawford Dillon and Arch Wheeler had been not just acquaintances but partners—and very good friends.

They'd struggled to launch a new magazine, Crawford supplying the business know-how, Wheeler the journalistic skills. It was hard-hitting, topical and tough, and they hoped it would also be commercial. They opened offices in New York, hired a staff—and lost money from the first issue. The critics were enthusiastic; the public wasn't. It was the wrong time.

Facing financial ruin, Crawford came up with the idea of changing the focus of *Modern Times*, making it a magazine of entertainment. He moved the offices to New Orleans, and to build up subscriptions and stimulate advertising, he initiated a revolutionary new idea—nudity in the pages of a respected national magazine. It had never been done before, and it succeeded beyond Crawford's wildest dreams. At last the time was right.

Crawford laughed softly. "You should have seen our 'shocking' magazine—a little nudity here and there from the waist up, some suggestive poses, a few sexual innuendos. Wouldn't be sneezed at today. But old Arch was livid. I promised to cut back on the nudity as soon as we got some good sales figures to take to our advertisers, but he wouldn't budge. Gave me one of his heavy lectures about how the end could never justify the means. Then he said I'd probably keep the nudity anyway, just out of spite."

"And he was right. You're still holding on to the centerfold," Jessica commented.

"I sure as hell am," Crawford swore. "Wheeler always was a sanctimonious son of a gun," he said with a grin. "He just reared up on his hind legs and marched out—after an argument you could have heard from New Orleans to New York. We said some mighty powerful things to each other." Crawford chuckled over the remembered scene of two angry young men, brash and self-righteous, who braved the publishing world and failed, searched for new horizons and finally broke up.

"'Course, I made his career," Crawford said, eyes twinkling. "He went into TV broadcasting and became a success."

"You did pretty well yourself," Jessica reminded him.

Crawford chuckled. "Yep," he agreed immodestly.

"You've been enemies ever since?" Jessica had left her spot on the stairs and settled in the comfortable porch swing. Crawford joined her, and they rocked back and forth—like two peas in a pod, Jessica expected him to say. He refrained.

"We aren't enemies," he said, "but we're certainly not friends. In fact, I don't reckon we've spoken to each other since then."

"I'd call that enemies," Jessica observed.

"No," Crawford responded. "I always nod when I meet him in public!"

"You're wary of Luke Maxwell because he's close to Arch Wheeler?"

"Let's just say the apple doesn't fall far from the tree," Crawford answered, not resisting the temptation to get an adage in this time. Jessica grimaced, and he ignored her. "I doubt if Wheeler would approve of his protégé seeing you—because of me. Wheeler thinks I'm an old reprobate and doesn't cotton to my evil ways. I'm not overly fond of his lofty ones, either."

"Luke is his own man, Crawford. He'll make his own decisions."

"So will you, goes without saying, but that doesn't

mean Wheeler won't be watching and disapproving just to be contrary. Luke's his fair-haired boy, a squeaky-clean version of the young Wheeler, cut in the same mold, he thinks. I've got a warning for Luke Maxwell: he'd better not betray Wheeler's trust."

"None of that has anything to do with Luke's relationship with me."

"Nope," Crawford agreed. "But just the same, Arch is not going to like it one little bit."

Jessica set her square chin in determination. "Like it or not, Luke and I have decided to see each other, no matter what anyone says."

Crawford chuckled and kept on swinging.

BUT SEEING EACH OTHER was more difficult than Luke or Jessica had realized. Far too often business trips kept her out of town, and on nights when she was in New Orleans, Luke was frequently at the studio late or involved in one of his growing number of speaking engagements. After one abortive attempt at an evening on the town, they set aside Sundays as their time together and spent them at the one place where no one could intrude—Luke's cabin.

He'd decided to begin the long-delayed work on the sleeping loft, and Jessica became a willing if untrained assistant. As they worked they talked, sometimes about their jobs but more often about their other interests. They'd both traveled extensively, and they discussed their trips, the music they enjoyed, books and even their favorite movies. Both were fans of Rachmaninoff, English mysteries, Bogart and a little town in France called Etrêtat. At first, they were surprised by these similarities in taste and then they began to take them for granted. It was becoming clear that they were very much alike. Their time together was easy and casual, filled with laughter and moments of affection.

"Who'd believe," he teased one sunny Sunday afternoon, "that Jessica Hale could hammer a nail with the best of them?" He climbed down from the loft and took Jessica in his arms.

"And who'd believe that Luke Maxwell would be found consorting with the naughty Jessica?" she retorted, returning his hug.

"No one," Luke responded, "except maybe the *Tattler*."

Jessica made a face. "Back to work, Maxwell; no more slacking off."

"You're quite a taskmaster," he complained.

She smiled sweetly. "How do you think I became head of Modern Times—because I knew the boss?"

"No comment," Luke said with a laugh as he pulled himself back up into the loft.

Late in the afternoon they rested under the trees before riding back to the house. Jessica leaned against the broad trunk of a magnolia while Luke sprawled on his back in the grass, his hands behind his head. Now in late May the blazing heat of summer was almost upon them. There'd only be a few days left like this, magically fresh with the final breath of spring. A dragonfly lazily circled Luke's head until Jessica waved it away with a careless swipe of her hand.

She leaned against the tree again, sighed and closed

her eyes, thinking about Luke. She seemed to think of him all the time now, not just when she was with him but when they were apart. His face filled her vision at the most inappropriate times—in the middle of meetings, during dictation to Toni, even in conference with Crawford. She'd made a point of taping "Speak Out" so she could watch at night curled up in bed. She admired the way Luke handled himself, asking probing questions his guests frequently tried to duck. She realized now that they were questions that needed to be asked—and answered.

Luke rolled over and stretched. "Looks like you have something important on your mind," he said.

"Not important at all," Jessica teased, "I was just thinking about you."

Luke laughed easily and propped himself on one elbow. "Any conclusions?"

"I think we've got a good thing going."

He smiled a slow lazy smile. "So do I, but I wish we could see each other more often."

"At least we have the phone," she reminded him.

"It's not the same." He reached out to touch her, and the touch proved his statement. They often talked on the telephone late at night, sharing the events of their busy crowded days. She looked forward to those calls; Luke Maxwell was becoming an important part of her life.

He got to his feet, brushed off his jeans, and held out his hand. "I hate to say this, but it's time for us to get back."

With a resigned sigh, Jessica put her hand in his and held on to him until they reached the horses.

Then Luke took her in his arms, pulling her close, rocking her gently.

"You feel so good in my arms, Jessica. Sometimes I don't want to let go."

Jessica knew the feeling all too well. She wrapped her arms around Luke's waist, holding on tightly, and tilted back her head to answer him. She didn't get the chance, for he used the opportunity to lean down and kiss her. His mouth made little circles on hers, his teeth nibbled at her lips, his tongue made probing forays against hers. It was a gentle kiss, warm, tender and passionate. Yet as gentle as it was, it shook her whole being. She pulled away, trembling and breathing erratically.

"You're quite a kisser, Mr. Maxwell," she whispered against his chest.

"That's only one of my fine qualities." He tried to joke, but his feelings were much too intense. "I want you, Jessica," he said. "I wonder if you know how much. I want more than kisses."

Jessica nodded. She had that same strong desire for him, and yet she still believed what she had told him earlier—she needed time; they both needed time.

Jessica wasn't the kind to rush headlong into intimacy, and she wasn't the kind to become just another woman in Luke Maxwell's life, remembered by nothing more than clothes left behind in a closet. Now that she cared for him, she was more determined than ever to wait until they were both sure of their feelings.

She stood on tiptoes and kissed Luke's cheek. "It'll happen when the time is right," she said.

Luke nodded. He was learning how to read Jessica, anticipate her needs and desires. She had changed from wary antagonist to delightful companion. He wanted more; he wanted her as his lover, but he wouldn't jeopardize that by frightening her away. Their relationship was changing, just as slowly and surely as spring was ripening into summer. She was a woman worth waiting for, and when she made her decision—he'd be there.

ON THURSDAY, WHEN JESSICA stepped out of her office at five past five, Toni glanced up, told herself she was seeing things, and went on typing. Jessica, purse slung over her shoulder, marched by her secretary's desk and headed for the elevator.

"I'm seeing things." Toni put her thoughts into words.

"You're not seeing things. I'm going home. Good night, Toni."

"If there'd been a death in the family, I'd have heard about it; short of that—"

Jessica stopped and turned, one hand resting on the navy stripe down the side of her white flannel skirt, a look in her eyes Toni couldn't interpret. "I came in an hour early; I took care of all the work; I'm going home. That's all." She thought the explanation quite satisfactory.

"That's not all," Toni said with a grin, her beautiful wide mouth curving deliciously and a little evilly. "Who is he? Tell, tell."

Jessica laughed and stepped into the elevator.

"I hope he's tall and handsome," Toni called after her.

"Definitely. And sexy," Jessica added just as the doors whooshed shut.

By six o'clock Jessica was standing in front of the open closet in the bedroom of her Garden District house. She rummaged through the closet once quickly with no results and then plopped into a corner chair. It was an antique, and it was in the wrong place, Jessica mused—a chair in a corner where no one sat. It was one of the many pieces of furniture she'd inherited from her father and crowded into the turn-of-the-century two-story house she'd bought the year before. Unfortunately, she'd never found the time to arrange the furniture and it remained where it had been unloaded—in the right rooms, but in the wrong places. It had never bothered her before; now it did. Luke had made her aware. While he managed so much else, Jessica could manage only her career.

Jessica stood up and returned to the closet. There hadn't been time for a nightlife, either, and now that she was faced with an evening of entertaining, she had nothing to wear. Then she remembered a dress she'd bought on a whim but never worn. She reached in the closet and pulled it out, a daring little strapless dinner dress. Just the thing. She undressed quickly, pulled on a pair of lacy gray stockings and wrapped the silk dress around her, hooking it in the back. She stepped into a pair of black ribboned very high heels and began to feel a lot better. Looking in the mirror, she decided on a glossy no-color lipstick, creating a unique look against her ivory-pale skin and a bold contrast with her dark brown hair, which Jessica suddenly decided to wear up, secured with an old-fashioned comb.

When Luke rang the bell at seven, she'd just finished setting the table and was still wrapped in a huge apron, which covered her skimpy dress completely.

"Two questions," he said as she led him into the house and past the dining room. "Are we eating here, and if so, can you cook?"

She started to answer, but he kept talking. "That was only one question—with two parts. Next is, do you have anything on under that apron?"

"Yes, yes and yes," she announced. "I decided to surprise you with dinner. I'm an excellent cook; in fact, I can do lots of things well."

"I'll bet." He smiled his wicked smile and leaned forward to kiss her lightly on the nose, but the kiss slid to her lips and wasn't light at all. It was deep and probing, not the kind of kiss to walk away from but the kind to cuddle into. They held each other afterward, and he whispered against her neck, "You feel so good." He kissed the curve of her neck at her collarbone where she'd applied an extra dab of perfume. "And taste so good," he said. "It's been a long time since our last date."

"Four nights," she reminded him.

"Much too long," he said, following her into the kitchen. "Now I remember—the night at the river. You made a terrific salad."

"I'm even better with seafood," she said, pulling up a stool and starting to butterfly a huge gulf shrimp from the bowl on the counter.

Luke made himself a drink and then stopped to watch her. "Can't get over it. My naughty lady is so domesticated. But I still don't know what—if anything—is under that apron."

"You'll see at dinner," she answered almost coyly.

"Nope," he said in a voice that was suddenly husky. "I'll see now." Jessica watched with surprise as he moved toward her. He reached out, lifted her from the stool, turned her around, untied the apron and pulled it off to reveal the black silk dress beneath.

He stepped back to have a better look. "Is it legal?"

"Barely," she answered with a smile.

He reached out and touched the row of lace at her breasts with curious fingers. She stood very still, hardly daring to breathe, watching him as he watched her. He ran his tongue over his lips and swallowed hard. "It's probably one of those dresses that looks simple but is as hard as hell to get out of."

"Not at all," Jessica said, breathing again. "There's just one hook in the back."

"Remind me of that when we get to your room," he murmured as he let his hand drop to encircle her waist. He pulled her, almost roughly, against him.

"The dinner—" she said.

"Later." His voice was emphatic. There was no arguing with it, not that she would have argued. Her need was as great as his.

"Oh, Jessica, I want you so much. Don't make me wait any longer."

She tried to answer, but her blood was ringing in her ears. She was as eager as he. "My bedroom's upstairs," she whispered as he picked her up lightly in his arms. "But there's a guest room down here."

"Even better," he murmured, thrilled by the note of husky desire in her voice. He carried her down the hall and into a little room that was lit by the soft glow of twilight. Putting her down in the middle of the room, Luke reached around her back for the hook. The dress dropped silently to the floor. He closed his eyes and took a deep breath. Jessica stood before him, wearing nothing but a wispy strapless bra, lacy stockings and high-heeled shoes. He reached out to touch her breasts. "Does this unhook?" he asked.

"Yes." She did it for him, and the bra fell to the floor on top of her dress. She stood before him with her full breasts heaving. He knelt down and took off her shoes and then, wrapping his arms around her legs, reached for the waistband of her panty hose and peeled them slowly down. Then he picked her up and placed her gently on the bed.

Jessica watched him as he undressed quickly, his eyes never leaving hers until he walked toward her, slim and masculine and filled with obvious desire. He stood above her for a long moment and let her look, and she drank in every part of his nude body, seeing for the first time what she'd imagined before—and she *had* thought about him without his clothes, Jessica admitted now to herself, but what she'd imagined was nothing compared to this trim bronzed figure who stood over her. She remembered the muscular forearms that had surprised her so when she first saw them. Now she saw them all—muscles that were long and tapered and sinewy, rippling in his arms and legs, in his hard lean hips and across his massive chest that was covered with soft hair. He bent over her, and she reached up to touch his chest and with both hands pull him down beside her on the bed.

This time when she removed his glasses there was no teasing left in her. They were both serious and they knew what they wanted, but as she moaned and softly pulled him close, hungry for his kisses and wanting more, much more, Luke was not to be rushed. He reached out and touched her hair first, finding the comb that held it in place, removing it to let her dark tresses fall loose around her shoulders so he could bury his face there and kiss the softness of her neck and shoulders.

Then his hands, which had been wrapped in her hair, traveled down across her ivory neck, across her shoulders to the soft contour of her breasts, her waiting breasts, her creamy breasts with nipples taut and rosy. He teased the pink rosettes between thumb and forefinger of each hand until she moaned in exquisite agony, and when his mouth found one and then the other, she cried out her desire. Trying to stem the cry, Jessica bit her lips until Luke noticed her silence. He lifted his head and spoke to her softly. "Cry out, Jessica. Say anything you feel." Then he kissed her, and parting her lips with his tongue, took her mouth in a way that sent shivers through every sensitive part of her body, causing her to throb with desire and need. It was a need he would not be long in fulfilling.

It was a need she could feel, for his hand had led her there, to the center of his male desire. Their kisses were deeper, longer, as if their lips could not bear to be apart. There was a wonder between them that they'd found each other and that such pleasure could exist. Jessica smiled into his kiss, and then they laughed and kissed again, but the laughter died as he rose high above her and entered her with a movement that was as sweet as it was sensual, joining with her in a quiver of ecstasy, neophytes on their first voyage of love together, learning the way as one.

There was perfection in their coupling, both in the giving and the receiving. Luke looked down at Jessica and smiled a smile so sweet and tender her eyes grew bright with sudden tears. She reached up to touch his face and the moment seemed suspended in time, she and Luke joined together . . . one.

The tempo of their lovemaking changed; the need became more urgent, the desire more powerful. With a glad little cry Jessica threw back her head, closed her eyes, giving herself to the wonderful sensations that coursed through her body and pounded in her veins and nerves and sinews.

"Luke, oh Luke." The words were wrung from her as together they came to their rapturous shuddering release.

They lay still afterward, holding each other, not yet able to speak.

There was no more glorious moment than this, Jessica thought, to be in the arms of her lover, safe, secure, satisfied, while their hearts slowed from the crescendo of their lovemaking. Her arms were wrapped around his body, once hot with desire, now cool and damp beneath her fingers.

Gently Jessica stroked his arm as if her touch could put into words what she was feeling for him. He'd been more than she'd hoped for, much more than she could have ever imagined. Jessica had known that she and Luke would make love, but she hadn't known it would be like this—as if she'd been given a rare and perfect gift. Because she couldn't put her feelings into words, she moved so she could kiss his cheek.

Luke smiled, opened his eyes and turned toward her, finding her lips and covering them expertly with his own, kissing her lovingly and very, very thoroughly. When at last the kiss was ended, Luke looked down at her, her face framed by her rich brown hair, eyes soft and mysterious from lovemaking, lips still swollen from his kisses.

"Some meal," he murmured.

"Let's plan another one soon," Jessica countered.

Luke lay back so she could snuggle against him again. "I wanted to make love to you the first time I saw you," he admitted, "in that sexy green dress—so cool and calm on the outside, so fiery underneath."

"And I wanted to kill you," Jessica said with a laugh.

"And now?"

"I think your idea is much, much better."

They rearranged themselves in each other's arms, too content to leave the bed and break the spell, and talked until the sky turned to black night and the moon rose over New Orleans.

She learned more about him in that long hour they spent together talking in bed than anyone she had ever known, not just his likes or dislikes, his hopes and dreams, but even his deep insecurities. All those escaped his lips in bed with Jessica that first night they made love.

"I have a confession," he said.

"A wife and six children."

He shook his head and idly played with a strand of her silky hair. "No. A confession of the conscience. I brought my prejudices to the show when you were on. I have never done that before, but I always knew it was possible."

"Why, Luke?"

"Because of my background. I let it get in the way. I didn't know much about your work but I knew something about you, your past, so different from mine. Even now I can still feel a bristling when I come up against someone like you—the silver-spoon crowd who grew up in wealth, attended private schools, did all those things that spell privilege and make me feel insecure."

Jessica sat up and leaned against the pillows, watching him as he talked.

"I went to public school, worked my way through the state university, fought for everything I ever got. I was grown before I ever went to a dinner party; before I felt comfortable at one and sure of which fork to use I was out of college. If I hadn't looked around that first time I spent a weekend in Newport, who knows what I would have done with the damned finger bowl."

Jessica giggled, but she knew he was serious.

"Some of the old insecurity—jealousy, by now—came through when I faced you that day. You were everything I wasn't."

Jessica snuggled up against him. "I suppose I did have it easy. My father was a successful lawyer, so was his father. . . ."

Luke nodded knowingly.

"But that didn't ease the pain when my mother died—I was only seven—or later when I lost my father."

"I'm sorry, Jessica, for being so self-centered." He hugged her close. "I'm sorry for your sadness."

"It's all right, Luke. It was a long time ago. What about your family?"

"I never really knew my father," Luke said. "He left home when I was three. My mother struggled to raise the family. I was the oldest, the first to leave home. I sent money to her until she died. I don't know what happened to my father."

"You must have been a very special child," Jessica said, "to have had the initiative to go so far. A Ph.D. . . . professorship at Tulane . . . hit television show. . . ."

"Sometimes I think I've put too much value on all that—on my reputation and image." He laughed deprecatingly. "But it's all I have. That and Arch Wheeler. He believes in me. He's encouraged me to—" Luke broke off.

"To what?" Jessica asked, curious.

"I'm interested in getting into politics."

Jessica wasn't really surprised when he said it. Luke was the kind of man who'd always have one more goal to reach. "Local? State?"

"U.S. Congress. Might as well aim high. I wasn't ready last election. I needed to build up more of a power base. . .I just wasn't ready. There's always the old insecurity."

"There's also the brilliance and authority and honesty. Those are certainly good traits where the electorate is concerned."

"I still have some time to think about it. If Arch has his way, I'll do it. But the choice is mine, and it's going to be a hard one that'll take some real soul-searching—on my own without Arch's prodding."

Jessica lay beside him quietly thinking. She wondered what Luke knew of Crawford and Wheeler. There was only one way to find out. She leaned up on one elbow and looked down into Luke's face. "Has your boss ever talked about Crawford?"

"Not that I remember. Why?" His brown eyes opened lazily and looked up at her.

"They used to know each other." Jessica decided not to tell him about the partnership. It was Wheeler's story, not hers. "Just ask him sometime," she said as she stretched languidly. "I think dinner's about two hours overdue."

Lazily they dressed, still touching, kissing, holding on to their special intimacy.

"Why don't I just take you out to dinner?" Luke suggested as he pulled on his shirt.

"No." Jessica ran her hands through his tangled hair, reached for his glasses on the bedside table and slipped them over the bridge of his nose. "Going out is too much of a hassle. Remember the time we tried?"

He nodded, remembering very well. They'd driven to Lake Pontchartrain, looking forward to a meal of soft-shelled crab and crawfish at one of the rambling restaurants that jutted out over the water. But when Luke stepped out of the car, a group of diners recognized him, shouted his name and started across the parking lot toward them.

"It's Luke Maxwell!" a voice called out.

"Who's with him—can you see in the car?"

Luke had clambered back in and quickly pulled out of his parking space. "So much—" he laughed "—for a quiet dinner."

They had ended up at a drive-in eating greasy hamburgers and laughing about the determined woman who'd pressed her face against the window trying to get a glimpse of Jessica. The laughter made it easier to take, but only in retrospect. Public curiosity was a very real threat to their personal lives.

Remembering, Jessica was filled with a sadness about what they were missing. She crossed the little bedroom and put her arms around his waist, hugging him tightly, her face against his chest, her lips pressed to the spot of bare skin where he'd missed a button on his shirt.

"You know what I'd like?" she said wistfully.

With a flourish he took off his glasses. "Dare I hope?"

Jessica grinned. "That goes without saying, but I'd like more. I'd like to have the things that lovers in New Orleans have—an evening of jazz, drinks at Top of the Mart, coffee and beignets in the Quarter, a walk around Jackson Square to look at the atrocious art. . . ."

. can do that," Luke said firmly. "All of it and ..."

ne looked up at him. "How? As soon as you show ur face, crowds—well, crowds of women, any-vay—gather around you like flies."

"I prefer a more pleasant image. How about bees to honey?"

Jessica laughed. "It might be pleasant for you, until they recognized me. Then we'd be in for a repeat of all that tawdry publicity. I don't want to make the cover of the *Tattler* again," she said emphatically.

Luke didn't answer at once. Instead he managed to shift her into the crook of his arm and finish buttoning his shirt before he announced casually, "You and I are going to the French Quarter Saturday night for dinner."

"Saturday night in the Quarter! You *are* crazy! Half of Louisiana will be there."

"Along with us. We'll have dinner and listen to jazz and go to the Café du Monde for coffee and beignets. . . ."

"Dream on."

"I'm not dreaming. This is for real." He bent down to kiss her cheek. "Stick with me, baby, and I'll make you. . .anonymous."

5

THE FOLLOWING SATURDAY an attractive couple stood patiently in the line that stretched down Bourbon Street, waiting with the crowd outside Galatoires. The woman tentatively touched her short blond curls and asked the tall man standing beside her, "Is my hair really—"

"Your hair is fine," he assured her. "I've always been partial to blue-eyed blondes."

"Don't get carried away; this is only for tonight."

"Well, for tonight, you're a great-looking blonde."

"How would you know? I bet all you can see is a blur."

"I can see every beautiful inch of you with my contact lenses. I just feel more well dressed with my glasses."

"And your public likes the image, which obviously works," she said, looking around at the other waiting customers, none of whom even glanced their way. "Without the glasses, you aren't Luke Maxwell. You probably didn't even need to change your hairstyle, even though it looks awfully cute," Jessica added. Luke's crisp dark hair, usually combed back from his face, was brushed forward over his forehead, a little messy and very appealing. Jessica had suggested the style, remembering Luke in the early-morning hours, boyishly unlike his public image. It was definitely a tousled bedroom hairstyle.

"So we'll be safe from the public—unless Miss Baton Rouge recognizes you. Or Miss Shreveport," Jessica had suggested lightly hours before when they were preparing the evening's disguises.

"Not in this fiendishly clever disguise," Luke responded. "Hey, what is this, anyway? A quiz about my past? Why don't you tell me about your old loves?"

"I prefer remaining a woman of mystery," Jessica had answered, fluffing the blond wig around her face and standing back from the mirror to admire the transformation.

"So you're going to be secretive," Luke said, not knowing how little there was to be secretive about in Jessica's life. Until Luke, no man had even begun to fill that empty space near her heart. Luke was different. He wasn't afraid of her power because he was even more powerful. Those still-lingering doubts about himself socially gave Luke a touch of humanity he'd seemed to lack when they first met. Face-to-face, he'd challenged her and emerged a winner. Now that power did not matter.

Except that it would have influenced their place in line outside Galatoires where they still waited patiently but watched a little jealously as a well-dressed couple breezed past to the front of the line, spoke a few words to the maître d' and were quickly ushered inside. Despite assurances that all patrons of Galatoires were treated equally—on a first-come first-served basis with no reservations accepted—it was well-known that concessions were made to long-time customers and celebrities. Both Luke and Jessica had benefitted from those concessions many times in the past. Tonight they were getting to see how the other half lived, and Jessica was getting impatient.

"If I wasn't wearing this damn wig," she complained, "we'd be halfway through dinner."

"Besieged by autograph seekers, photographers and all the New Orleans curious. You were the one who didn't want to go public," he reminded her. "Anyway, isn't this more fun?" He put his arm around her and pulled her close.

There was something about Luke tonight that was different, here in the street with the rest of the crowd, unrecognized. It was a warmth that had a fun-loving spirit in it, a wittiness, a charm. The celebrity had disappeared and the very personable man remained, a serious man, intense and very intelligent. Each time she was with him, Jessica discovered something new, as if he'd taken off one hat to reveal another beneath it, then another and another. He was a complex man who was playful, and by the time they reached the front of the line she'd caught his spirit and was delighted when the bored waiter, who offered no more than a cursory glance in their direction, seated them at a table that was far from the best, not the table that Luke Maxwell of "Speak Out" or Jessica Hale of Modern Times would have rated.

"It's better," she declared. "Quieter, out of the limelight." She gave his knee an intimate little nudge. "Secluded."

"See, it pays to be anonymous."

Jessica agreed as she looked around the elegant old restaurant with its black-and-white tiled floors and the lazily swirling ceiling fans she'd often sat beneath with Crawford or with business associates or important New Orleanians. She planned to enjoy herself tonight as never before, and she *did* as they dined extravagantly on the rich sautéed crab and crispy French bread slathered with butter, washed down with dry white wine.

Hours later, after taking their time in spite of unfriendly glances from the management, Jessica sipped the rich black chicory coffee and reached spontaneously for Luke's hand. "What next?" she asked. "I'm ready for anything."

"Then come on and prove it," Luke challenged as they left the restaurant and stepped into nighttime New Orleans, moving along carefully through streets closed to traffic. Locals and tourists on their way to Pat O'Brien's and Pete Fountain's brushed shoulders with teenagers squeezed into designer jeans, carefully coiffed senior citizens, a sprinkling of transvestites, the remnants of a motorcycle gang, debutantes and ladies of the night. It was part carnival, part parade. It was Saturday night in the French Quarter, and Jessica and Luke, holding hands with disguises in place, joined the wild eclectic mixture.

When midnight had passed and morning had taken its place, when they'd seen and tasted and felt all of the Quarter two people could digest in one enthusiastic gulp, they found themselves in a smoky club on Bourbon Street listening to a jazz pianist and drinking Sazeracs. Something else was in the air now. The excitement had slowly died and they had become more intensely aware of each other.

Their eyes met through the smoke over their untouched drinks in the hot closeness of the bar. They no longer heard the piano. Part of yesterday, it was over. Luke reached for Jessica's hand and they got up together and walked back to the car through the quiet streets that held only memories of the night's gaiety. Their arms were around each other as they walked toward the car, stopping to kiss once long and passionately under a wrought-iron balcony. Faintly from inside the building came the plaintive moan of a lone clarinet, but they didn't really hear it. There was only one emotion left them now, and that was the overpowering need for each other.

Luke raced his car through the streets to Jessica's house where they made love wildly, passionately and with the spellbinding release of two who had followed a night of excitement with a morning of ecstasy.

When they awoke toward noon, Luke said sleepily but seriously, "We need more of this, Jessica. More times like last night when we can be together and go places and do things with the rest of the world. Let's go public. Let's do whatever the hell we want from now on." He pulled her close, capturing her with a bronzed arm so that her head could rest on his shoulder. His thigh was molded against hers; her arm was flung across him; her fingers made patterns in the featherings of dark hair on his chest.

"Whatever we want to do. . . ." Jessica almost

agreed, and then a memory invaded her mind. She thought of them walking through the streets of the French Quarter anonymously, no one asking questions, no one taking pictures. They'd been a man and a woman like any other, sharing a night. Jessica didn't want that to end. "Not yet, Luke. Please. Let's hold on to what we have at least for a while without the insinuations and questions. Just us."

"You're sure?"

"Yes," she responded without hesitation, snuggling even closer to the warmth of his body. "I'm sure."

"Okay," he said firmly, "then we'll go away together where we don't have to hide behind disguises. Where I can put on my glasses again," he said with a grin. "China? India? Spain? Russia?" Luke sang out, becoming more enthusiastic with each exotic suggestion.

Jessica kissed his cheek and laughed at his fervor. "I have an idea," she suggested seriously. "Much simpler and more realistic. Mexico. There're direct flights from New Orleans International. . . ." She wiggled excitedly and caused a little gasp to escape Luke's lips as her breasts brushed suggestively against his chest.

"Sounds like the perfect place, Jessica. Just say when."

"Next week," she answered spontaneously and then moaned. "What are we talking about? You have a show and I'm due in Chicago next week." Brow furrowed, she frowned unhappily into Luke's face.

"Think, Jessica. There's a way to do this. What about the following week?"

"Nothing scheduled yet." Her voice was tentative but hopeful.

"Then close the book. Don't make any commitments." Luke wrapped his arms around her and pulled her on top of him. He felt her satiny smooth skin, he saw her face glow with excitement, and he wanted desperately to kiss her full ripe mouth, but Jessica rolled away and sat up against the pillows. She was totally involved in her plans.

"I'll need a few days to clear up things at the office." She was beginning to realize her dream was possible. "But what about you?"

The sheet was pulled carelessly over Jessica's breasts creating a provocatively innocent pose. Luke's hand moved under the covers to glide along her thigh, skim over her rounded hip and come to rest on the flat plane of her stomach. "I'll think of something," he said, closing his eyes and luxuriating in the feel of her skin beneath his caressing hand.

Jessica caught her breath, very conscious of his warm seeking hand but also determined to finish the plans about their vacation. "You can't just walk away from 'Speak Out.'"

"True," he answered, "but I can tape a week ahead."

It *was* possible, Jessica realized. "Won't it be wonderful? All alone in Mexico, swimming in clear blue water under soft tropical breezes. . . ."

Luke laughed. "You're getting carried away, Jessica. What really matters is no phone calls and no interruptions. Don't mention our plans. No one on your staff—or even Crawford Dillon—is going to interrupt my time alone with you."

"It's a deal," Jessica agreed. "No one will know where we're going."

With a quick movement Luke pulled Jessica close and pinioned her body beneath his. He could no longer ignore his arousal, not when Jessica was here beside him so flamboyantly sensual—and hardly aware of the devastating effect she'd created.

She looked up with laughing eyes. "By the way, where are we going?"

"Mexico was your idea. I thought you knew—"

"I've never been there," she admitted.

"I, on the other hand, have been there lots of times," Luke said, placing a kiss on her neck. "And I know—" he paused again to kiss her eyelids "—the perfect place." His lips touched her nose and then hovered a millimeter from her mouth. "Where no one will ever find us."

Jessica smiled trustingly and raised her mouth to meet his. Their plans complete, she lost herself in the wonder of Luke.

"YOU'RE GOING ON VACATION? Will wonders never cease." Toni sat across from Jessica taking notes as fast as her boss could dictate. "Where to?"

"That," said Jessica, "is a state secret."

"Well, I might not know where, but I sure do know who," Toni said, putting down her steno pad and forgetting about the Chicago sales force. "It's the mystery man, right?"

Jessica shrugged, and Toni frowned. This was a new Jessica, zealously guarding her private life.

"So at least tell *me* where you're going in case there's an emergency."

Jessica shook her head. "No emergencies allowed, Toni. I have complete faith in my department heads and my assistant. You'll handle anything that comes up."

"What about Mr. Dillon? You've got to tell him," Toni insisted.

"No." Jessica laughed. "I don't believe I'm saying this, but not even Crawford will know the secret spot." Jessica thought briefly about that statement. Never had she left MT without giving Crawford all the numbers where she could be reached, including those en route, and she'd always called him several times during her trips and even her vacations. She wondered if she was going to be able to keep this pledge, and she also wondered what in the world had possessed her to make it. She *knew* what possessed her. It was Luke. He had the power to make her forget everything when she was in his arms, even when she was just thinking of being in his arms.

"Well," Toni said, probing, "this guy must be pretty special, whoever he is."

Toni was rewarded for her persistence with a single word. "Yep." That was all she would get.

JESSICA FLEW INTO CABO SAN LUCAS from Mexico City still wearing her blond wig used for the "getaway" in New Orleans. She'd keep on the disguise until she and Luke were together on their way to Santa Isabella. Better not take any chances, she had decided.

The decision was a wise one. The airport at Cabo San Lucas was filled with Americans, rich Americans, Jessica noticed after a careful look, all converging at the tip of the Baja Peninsula to take advantage of the marlin fishing, the deluxe hotels, the good food and interesting nightlife. There were even American kids dressed in the casual clothes of the wealthy, here on a surfing vacation in the land where perfect dark blue waves rose slowly from the clear turquoise Pacific. This was surfing and fishing country. And it was beautiful.

Jessica took her time walking through the thatched-roof airport, sure that she'd landed in paradise. The air was hot but not humid; the heat built and then dissipated when the desert met the sea. It was perfect, clear and crisp. Almost laughing in delight as she emerged from the open bamboo hut, Jessica headed for the taxi stand in the afternoon sun and added her name to the list of waiting travelers. She spent an anticipatory ten minutes before her name was called during which her heart pounded in expectation of the adventure ahead.

"Get a taxi ride out of town on the coastal road toward Santa Isabella," Luke had told her. "I'll be waiting."

When her name was called, Jessica headed for her taxi with a little thrill. This was like something out of the movies, its romance intensified by its mystery. She clambered into the old cab like a schoolgirl, forgetting that she had to give directions to the dispatcher. As he leaned over and poked his head through the window, Jessica repeated Luke's instructions, which were passed on to a puzzled driver who knew some English, but not enough to ask why this American woman was heading north with no apparent destination. Shrugging, he put the car into gear and started off. She would tell him, he understood, when the time came to stop.

As they drove through town, Jessica was momentarily disillusioned. It was one big fair with shops jammed against each other selling everything from low-priced tequila to high-priced T-shirts emblazoned with Cabo San Lucas, pottery, tiles and gaudy plaster of paris and papier-mâché artifacts in varying degrees of worthlessness. There was a feeling of harassment in the air, with too much being offered and too little being sold. Just another tourist trap, she decided, more colorful than some but of no more interest.

They escaped the town and climbed high above the turquoise sea on the winding road that hung precipitously between the hot high desert and the cool Pacific, and Jessica realized her first impression was correct. This was paradise, and she was going to share it with Luke—wherever he was.

She kept her eyes on the road ahead, looking away toward the sea only when the view was too breathtaking to resist. They drove for miles until the traffic thinned out as other taxis and rental cars turned off at hotels and condominiums along the road toward Santa Isabella. Jessica began to get nervous. Suppose something had happened and Luke didn't appear?

She had no idea what his plans were. Luke had been very cautious and mysterious, telling her little except that she'd find him, and together they'd journey to their destination. Well, it had better be soon, Jessica thought as they climbed another steep incline and the little taxi began to sputter. This was probably the longest journey from Cabo San Lucas the cab had made in years.

Then she saw a car in the distance, stopped along the road, a figure standing beside it. She called out to the driver and pointed, asking him in her rudimentary Spanish to slow down. As they got closer she recognized Luke. He was leaning against the dusty car, which had been black once and new once but was neither of these now. One hand rested on the hood, the other was shoved into the pocket of khaki pants. He was wearing clip-on sunglasses over his horn-rims, and he looked to Jessica like the most romantic figure she'd ever seen. The old taxi screeched to a halt and Luke opened the door, took out her bag, and reached for her hand. "Going my way?"

Laughing, Jessica fell into his arms. She had the feeling this was the beginning of a dream vacation.

"This part of the world boasts no-status car rentals," Luke explained as he paid the taxi driver and settled Jessica into the old Volkswagen.

"I don't care," she answered with a glowing smile. "This car seems just right; I feel I'm living a romantic old movie."

"Wait till we get to Santa Isabella. You'll begin to think you're Ingrid Bergman and I'm—"

"Humphrey Bogart!"

Luke turned to her with a sexy smile. "Here's looking at you, kid."

With a laugh she pulled off the wig and tossed it onto the back seat of the car. She shook her long, brown hair free and turned to Luke with a look that said she was ready for anything.

They drove away slowly, almost reluctant to reach their destination, sure that it could not equal their hopes for it. At first they thought they were right as they neared Santa Isabella after dark. It was a sleepy village—night and day—Luke told Jessica. Then he was surprised to see how the little town had changed, its main street paved now, two new hotels nestled elegantly on the beach.

"What I see is not what I remember," Luke said, a little disappointed.

"How long has it been?"

"A long time, I admit," he answered, looking around. "I came here for vacation the first year I taught at Tulane. There weren't any hotels here except the Parador del Sol. I'm afraid that Santa Isabella's been discovered. Let's just hope the appeal is for serious marlin fishermen instead of tourists."

He turned the car and headed up the hill. At the end of a winding road they stopped beside the Parador del Sol. A sleepy desk clerk signed in *Señor* Maxwell and *Señorita* Hale and an even sleepier bellboy carried the luggage to their room.

"The hotel is just the same," Luke whispered to her as they climbed the stairs behind the bellboy. There was excitement in his voice. This was Luke's discovery, and just as he'd made the place his own years before, now he wanted to share it with Jessica. It would be special for them; his voice and the touch of his hand told her that.

When they were alone, Luke opened the double doors and led her onto the balcony. The air was warm and still, redolent with the scent of flowers. The sky was an ebony blanket sprinkled with a scattering of stars and a full moon rode high in the black night.

Jessica slipped her arms around Luke's waist. "It's perfect."

He kissed her once gently and said, "I'm glad you're pleased. I have good memories of it, but the memories of this trip will be even better." He turned her head toward him, tilting her chin up with the tips of his fingers. Then he kissed her lightly on the lips, and they turned together arm in arm, walked back into their room, leaving the doors open to let the night follow them to their bed.

WHEN JESSICA WALKED OUT of the dressing room, Luke was already in bed, his nude body partially covered by the sheet. He gave a low whistle as she moved into his line of vision. He'd never seen the nightgown she was wearing. She'd bought it for the trip—for him, and that pleased him. It wasn't a gown, really, he thought, just the suggestion of one, covering her from barely above her full breasts to. . . . He looked again, and as he looked she turned, and he saw that the gown just reached below the firm line of her bottom. It was black and filmy and very sexy.

"Words fail me, Jessica."

She'd felt a little brazen when she first put on the gown, but she approached the bed almost shyly. They'd made love before many times, but this was different. Now they were making a commitment to each other for a week—to spend every day together, to sleep together every night. She was a little nervous about being with him. What would it be like? Would this vacation herald a new beginning? Luke read the emotions on her face and held out a hand for her.

"Come beside me, Jessica." He drew her down to the bed so he could hold her close. He buried his head in the silky skin between her shoulder and neck, licking gently with his tongue, nipping lightly with his teeth. He felt her tremble and held her even more tightly.

"You're so beautiful," he whispered. "I want you just as much. . . ." He kissed her lips softly. "No, more than ever," he amended. "Tonight will be a wonderful night, my love. Our first night in Mexico."

Gently he drew the gown up over her head so that she lay nude on the sheet beside him. Her ivory-soft skin glowed in the light that trickled in through the open balcony doors; her hair shone like cinnamon fire.

"We're going very slowly tonight," he whispered. "I want to taste and touch every inch of you. Every delicious inch."

Jessica sighed under the spell of his voice and his hands. He reached for her breasts and cupped them, urging her tender nipples to rub against his palms. At his touch Jessica felt a warm melting sensation flow through her, as if she were honey softening under the sun. While his hands caressed her breasts, Luke's mouth trailed kisses on her face, her neck, her shoulders. His tongue ran hungrily along her flesh, leaving a moist reminder of his passing.

"You taste so good, Jessica. So sweet that I want more."

His mouth moved to her breasts, and slowly, sensually played a magic symphony upon the taut pink buds. Using mouth and tongue, he made Jessica writhe beneath him. She called out his name and wrapped her fingers in his hair, holding his mouth to her breast—just a little longer, longer!

With a groan Luke rolled over. He'd meant to go slowly; he'd meant to tease and tantalize, but just being near Jessica aroused him until he was aflame with her.

It was her turn now, her turn to play wanton. Her hands found his male nipples, touched them, caught them between her fingers until Luke shivered from the pleasure she gave. She doubled that pleasure by using her mouth and tongue, delighting that he was as responsive as she.

Her hands slid down his flat stomach and found his manhood, hard and eager. She caressed him, tentatively at first and then more boldly, spurred on by his sounds of ecstasy.

"I want to give you pleasure, Luke," she whispered. "I want to touch you and give you pleasure."

His answer was a low moan as he pulled her face downward to his open mouth. They kissed for a long time, tongue seeking tongue, as hands explored, sought, found and caressed. Here, the smooth roundness of a breast; there, the hard line of a rib. His lips discovered the soft skin at the base of her stomach, inside her thigh, behind her knee. He kissed her in each place to her tremulous delight.

Theirs was a search that had no beginning and no ending. She adored the hands that trailed hot fire across her flesh; he loved each part of her he touched and tasted. Her tongue probed the smooth recesses of his ear as his fingers found the warm moistness between her legs.

They could wait no longer. He claimed her as his own, his Jessica, whose body drove him wild with delight. She let herself be claimed and then asserted her own needs, enfolding his maleness within her and drawing from him the essence of his love. Their senses clamored for release as they moved together in the hot tropical night, aware of nothing except their own needs. The ocean roared, the moon raced across the sky and the night birds sang out. They neither heard nor saw any of this, for their release was near, so near. At last it came, and they were fulfilled—completely. Then they slept, still holding each other, still warm with the love they'd shared.

In the morning they walked around the Parador del Sol, and Luke was relieved to see that it was still the gracious old hotel he remembered—freshly whitewashed adobe walls, red-tile roof glowing in the sun, fountains splashing musically in a garden vibrant with the flowers of summer. It was quiet, not well-known and rarely publicized. The owners preferred it that way, each season welcoming the American fishermen and the British and Canadian tourists who frowned upon inflated prices and overcrowding in the glamour spots of Mexico.

After breakfast Luke and Jessica walked hand in hand down the winding path toward the village, emerging from the arid palms and cactus plants above an oasis. It was a well-populated, commercial oasis.

"There's my remote paradise in the light of day," Luke said, disappointed. They stood on the hill looking down at the village, which had burst its seams with a string of restaurants stretching along the main street, hotels and condos in a parallel line—all stucco symbols of progress marching along the beach.

Luke shook his head, made an abrupt turn and, pulling Jessica along after him, started down the rocky hillside toward the beach below. "Looks like progress is headed south, so we're going north." Their feet touched the sugar-soft sand and reassured them nothing could ruin the beauty of this perfect little bay washed by the turquoise water of the Pacific, cool and crystal clear. They roamed the solitary beach until Jessica talked him into a shopping trip. Once in town, taking his cue from her enthusiasm, Luke decided to buy Jessica a present. "I consented to go shopping so I'll buy you something to mark the occasion."

"You didn't exactly consent. You were dragged," Jessica said. She poked among the bright cotton clothes that filled the racks of every little store while Luke carefully examined a tray of silver-and-turquoise bracelets. Jessica shook her head as he held up each choice. She'd found what she wanted. A white dress with puffed sleeves and a scooped neckline, the cotton interspersed with lace falling in graceful layers to the floor. She stepped behind a curtain to try it on.

"Ah, *señorita*, so...so...*bonita*," the enthusiastic proprietor declared. "This dress is for you. It is...it is like a wedding dress."

Jessica hesitated, avoided Luke's gaze and looked at her reflection in the mirror. "Perhaps," she mumbled, "I should forget it."

"Not on your life," Luke answered, his eyes flicking with the intensity of a camera shutter, recording the image of Jessica's radiant face above the white dress. "The dress is yours," he added softly.

By the time they reached the end of the street they were loaded down with presents for Toni, Crawford, Arch Wheeler—all great fun to buy and all completely useless. They fell onto a wooden bench at an outdoor restaurant and demolished a huge meal beginning with margaritas and ending with puff-pastry *sopaipillas* and Mexican chocolate.

Just as they took their last sips of chocolate, a bus pulled into the square. Tourists poured off like soldiers ready to do battle with their cameras, and were further fortified with wide-brimmed hats, straw bags and boundless energy. As they dispersed and headed toward the shops, two of the women, faces serious and intent, ready for combat, broke away from the crowd and headed toward the restaurant.

Jessica instinctively put on her sunglasses and Luke

lowered his head and put on a garish sombrero he'd bought as a joke for his director. Then they looked at each other and laughed.

"Old habits die hard," Luke said, grabbing her hand, "but let's get out of here just in case. . . ."

They waited at the cash register while the owner chatted with friends and lackadaisically considered taking their money, which gave the hawkeyed women time to jockey for a place with a better view.

"I say it *is* him," a voice drifted toward their carefully turned but hardly inconspicuous backs.

The other woman disagreed. "Luke Maxwell would never be dressed so disreputably in shorts and a T-shirt—and that ridiculous hat," she said assuredly.

Her friend considered this and then let go with a challenge. "*She* could be Jessica Hale, you know, the one who runs that magazine and used to be involved with her boss."

Jessica flinched perceptibly at that remark while Luke's face remained unreadable.

"Certainly not," the doubting one countered. "Jessica Hale is much better looking!"

Jessica and Luke finally paid the bill and managed to get out of the restaurant and into the street before their laughter exploded.

THE NEXT DAY THEY DROVE the old VW north from Santa Isabella to a village so small that the handful of fishermen who lived there had never bothered to give it a name. Luke pulled off the road beside a row of wooden boats lying idle in the afternoon sun. Three men squatted beside the boats, talking softly. They barely looked up when Luke and Jessica passed with their towels and picnic basket.

"That's the kind of impression I like to make," Luke said with a smile.

They continued across the wide pebbly beach and found a smooth spot a few yards from the retreating tide. Luke stripped to his bathing suit, handed Jessica his glasses and headed for the surf with a careless challenge for her to join him. Jessica took one look at the surf, recalled the gentle waves in the gulf and refused, shaking her head firmly. "It's not my idea of fun to be pounded to death by eight-foot breakers."

She stretched out in the sun and watched Luke as he plunged into a wave and came up swimming, his strokes long and even. She mused that he'd probably taught himself to swim as he'd taught himself to ride, with sheer grit and determination. She watched fascinated as he took the first wave, threw his body forward, feet fluttering and one hand raised high until he caught the crest, stretched out and rode across it with an elegant strength that caused her to hold her breath. Then he disappeared in the white water to emerge again way out at sea, poised and waiting for the next good wave. A smile curved her lips as she tucked a rolled towel under her head, reached into her big canvas bag and pulled out a yellow pad and a felt pen. She started to write, glancing up occasionally to watch his brown body ride another wave.

Jessica's eyes were closed and her head nestled against the towel half an hour later when a shadow fell across her and blocked the hot sun. She seemed to feel the darkness but didn't open her eyes until he shook the chilly water from his hair and shoulders over her bare stomach. Then she threw a handful of sand, but it totally missed the mark. Laughing, Luke reached into his bag for his glasses, put them on and stared at her as if in surprise.

"Is it. . . could it be Jessica Hale of Modern Times?" He stood above her looking down to scrutinize her flushed face, her expression still a little drowsy, hair hanging loose around her shoulders, eyes made bluer by her tan and more sparkling by the sight of him. If he was pleased with what he saw, so was Jessica. His muscular body was always a surprise, even more here on the beach, wet and glistening in the bright sun.

Luke shielded his eyes, looked at her again carefully and then said, "No, it couldn't be Jessica Hale. She's much better looking."

At Jessica's pretended anger, he fell to his knees beside her, leaned forward and kissed her once, twice, three times while she savored the sweet warmth of his lips tinged with the salty sea. The wind caught her hair and blew it across his face. He laughed and held her close. Then he noticed the yellow pad beside her.

"No work allowed," he censured.

"It's not work" was her vague response as she tossed the pad—turned quickly face down—into the sand.

"What then?" Luke stretched out beside her, reaching for the pad.

"I'm not telling," she said, pushing it farther away. "A woman deserves some privacy."

Luke left the pad in the sand, but his curiosity was whetted. "Letters to an old lover?"

She closed her eyes as if deep in thought and finally said, almost shyly, "Poetry."

"Poetry?" he repeated.

"Well, don't act so amazed," she began defensively. "I started writing in college and was considered quite a poetess." She leaned back against him and bragged a little. "I was published in national student collections."

A grin crossed Luke's lips. "Another surprise from this surprising woman. Horseback . . . poetry . . . ."

"All part of my past. It's strange," she said, reaching up to touch his shoulder, warm from the sun. "You made me remember what it was like before I got so involved in work. I'm glad to have it all brought back again."

Luke looked over at her—the sophisticated Jessica Hale, hard driving, successful, here on a beach in Baja talking almost shyly about her poems.

He turned over the pad and handed it to her. "Read me your poem, Jessica," he said in a voice tender with emotion.

She hesitated, and then quietly her low soft voice floated across the hot summer air.

"The ocean sends shock waves
Toward the waiting, hesitant shore
Giving notice to the endless stretch of sand,
Doubtful, challenging, holding out for more."

Luke lifted one eyebrow. "What does it mean?"

"I have no idea!"

"Well," he said, pulling her close beside him and covering her with his damp sandy body. "It *sounds* good."

6

JESSICA STRETCHED OUT HER HAND, reaching for her iced drink, but instead of a cold glass she encountered a warm arm, then a shoulder and neck. She rolled over, sat up and took off her sunglasses.

"You drank my Piña Colada!"

Luke, stretched beside her near the hotel pool, kept his eyes closed. "'Course I drank it. You left it within reach, and I'd already finished mine."

Jessica started to respond to that crazy reasoning, but it was too hot so she simply nodded and lay back on the towel. "There's nothing left but the condensation," she managed to say with a sad look at the empty glass. Then an even sadder thought intruded, "And we only have two more days!"

Luke opened one eye and laughed at her woebegone expression. "Look at it this way, Jessica: Isn't it great that we still have two more days? And two nights," he added suggestively, raising one eyebrow.

It was Jessica's turn to laugh at his expression of lust. "Try to behave, Luke. We aren't alone." Across the pool another couple was braving the afternoon sun.

"Well, we're all crazy to be out in this heat." He sat up and glanced at his watch. "Two o'clock and hot as Hades. Let's go inside. It's bound to be cooler."

The hotel *was* cooler, insulated against the sun by thick walls, high ceilings and a heavy tile roof. Luke took a quick shower, toweled off and fell naked across the clean sheets on their big double bed, situating himself directly under the rotating ceiling fan. "That's more like it," he sighed, closing his eyes.

Jessica looked at him enviously and headed for the shower. As she stood immobile under the cooling spray, she thought about their vacation. It had been an idyll in which Modern Times vanished with civilization itself. Over a thousand miles from New Orleans, they were a million miles from its problems with no radio or TV to jar them back to reality. And they hadn't even bothered to open a newspaper. Since the first day when they were almost recognized, there'd been no more incidents. Occasionally an American tourist would give them an inquisitive glance, but with Luke in shorts and a T-shirt and Jessica in one of her large selection of wildly printed sundresses with her hair tied back, they were just another couple on holiday. Sunglasses hid her startling blue eyes, and although her style of dress was original and exciting, even a little sexy with the plunging necklines, it did not do more than turn a few male heads. There was nothing special about Jesisica and Luke except the special way they looked at each other.

It had been idyllic, in spite of the mounting heat, with long mornings on the beach, lazy afternoons making love, talking, laughing together, getting to know each other, opening up as neither had ever done before. Their time together, though brief, had been intense. They'd explored each other thoroughly. She'd looked into every corner of his mind and touched every part of his body.

But it was Luke's exploration of Jessica that startled her. No one had ever come so close—not even Crawford—to learning the secrets of her heart. Luke knew her as she'd never expected to be known, and she felt released. He shared her thoughts and feelings deeply, with every one of the senses, and that made her reel. It was too overpowering to understand. She turned off the shower at last and, wrapped in a towel, went back into the bedroom. Luke was asleep.

Jessica sat on the edge of the bed and thought about the lazy afternoon that stretched before them and the long evening that would follow, beginning at the little café in the hills. They'd become regulars there, greeted by the owner, hovered over by the waiter and serenaded by a vivacious guitarist. One night Luke had taken up the guitar and begun to play to everyone's delight and Jessica's surprise.

"I've never played in public in my life," he admitted to Jessica later. "Don't know what possessed me."

"There was a guitar in your room at the house," Jessica said thoughtfully. "I just assumed it belonged to someone else."

"Haven't played in years."

"I haven't written poetry in years."

"We're changing, Jessica."

Her thoughts, as she sat beside him on the bed, seemed to make their way to Luke, who opened his eyes and held out his arms. Overhead, the fan whirled, creating a breeze, which, although it was warm, was somehow tempting. His long form stretched on the sheets was even more tempting, the tan deeper than ever.

"It's too darn hot," she said, not meaning the words, for her desire was greater now in the extreme heat, somehow intensified. There was a pitcher of water beside the bed. She eyed it wickedly. "We just need a little cooling off," she said, picking it up and holding it above his supine body.

"Jessica—"

"Too late." She giggled as she started to sprinkle the water over his chest.

Luke reached up and grabbed the pitcher, splashing the remains upward. She dropped the towel when she tried to move out of the way and got the full force of the water across her naked body.

"You. . .you. . . ." Both of them, dripping under the whirling fan, burst out laughing. He dropped the empty pitcher to the floor and pulled her down beside him. She was aware of his desire and her own need was instantaneous, provoked by the heat and the pleasure of his touch.

Luke's eyes glided over Jessica as she lay languidly beside him, laughing and relaxed, the drops of water gleaming on her skin like dew on the petals of a flower. He leaned over and covered her lips with his, kissing the finely etched upper lip, then the lower, full and sensual, then the corners of her mouth. As she opened her lips in pleasure his tongue sought hers, exploring the silken hidden interior of her mouth with little darting movements.

All of Jessica's senses were alive and crying out for

fulfillment. Above her she heard the faint hum of the fan, felt its soft breeze stir her hair, and all around her was the sweet heady scent of flowers. Luke's hands and mouth worked their magic on her, and in between the kisses his voice whispered delicious loving words.

"You're so beautiful, Jessica, so soft and satiny. You seem to glow when I touch you." She did. Jessica could feel the glow. Her heart smiled along with her lips, and she was filled with happiness—and love.

His tongue traced a path of moist warmth to Jessica's breast and slowly licked a drop of water from the creamy skin. He raised his head and gave her a look melting with desire before his mouth claimed the eager pink bud of her nipple. Jessica cried out—not for him to stop—but to continue this overwhelming assault on her senses.

As his tongue tasted and teased, she stretched out against his long hard length, her hands moving greedily over his body. She seemed to be touching him for the very first time, discovering the powerful muscles of his back, the line of his spine, the hard plane of his stomach and finally the bold evidence of his desire. Lovingly she caressed him, oblivious to anything but the feelings surging through her and his masculine strength in her hands.

His mouth found her other breast as his hand snaked down and around her body, exploring her back and buttocks and then touching expertly and tantalizingly the center of her desire. Jessica's hands moved too, circling his back and tightening, and her voice became breathless as she urged him to go on . . . and on.

Her sigh was one of delight as Luke's mouth moved lower, tracing with his tongue the circle of her navel, nibbling on her hipbone with gentle teeth and then tasting the soft skin inside her thigh. She held her breath—waiting. . . waiting until Luke's mouth sought and found at last the honeyed secrets of her passion.

Ripples of pleasure streaked through her so powerfully, so movingly that Jessica was sure she'd explode into a million pieces and be swept away on the breeze. She twisted under him, wanting to break away from the delicious torment, but Luke wasn't ready to let her go, not when his hands could cup her full lush breasts or his mouth give her pleasure so intense she cried out to him.

"Please," she almost begged. "Please. Now!"

Luke was ready, more than ready, to enter her and claim her as his own. She raised her hips to meet him eagerly, ardently, so that they came together as one. There was no need for slowness now, no need for teasing, no need to hold back what they both had longed for.

They moved in elemental rhythm, bodies slippery one upon the other. Jessica wrapped her slim legs around Luke's back so she could be closer, closer, striving to become part of him, part of the man to whom her heart and body cried out so wildly. Hot fire pumped through veins as their movements became more swift, more fierce, until at last together they found release. Sweet rapture triumphed as they cried out in unison their pleasure and love.

A moment passed, an hour, a day—she couldn't be sure. Jessica lay beside him burying her face in his passion-wet body. There were no words, not even any thoughts left now. There was only Luke, and she clung to him.

The fan dried their moist bodies as they slept and woke and slept again in each other's arms. The sun was setting and the long-awaited breeze from the sea had sprung up when they lazily emerged from their cocoon of pleasure. There was no way to describe what had happened between them. They didn't even try.

Showering together later under the cool spray, they held each other silently, her face nestled against his chest, letting the water wash softly over them. It was a gentle time with passion spent, a time to be together with no need for words. As they dried off and began to dress, Luke smiled at Jessica and brought them back to reality.

She'd pulled on a bright red hip-hugging cotton skirt with a long slit up the side. Luke nodded appreciatively. "Let's eat at our place tonight."

"Only if you promise to play the guitar."

He tried to look modest. Then he started to laugh. "Will you guarantee that Pedro and the customers won't start throwing things?"

"I guarantee," she said, putting on a printed blouse she'd bought at one of the little shops in town. "You play beautifully." The blouse had a drawstring around the neck, which she didn't get a chance to tie. Luke had reached out to stop her, pulling the blouse down over her breasts. Her skin was still cool from the shower, but her nipples turned hot and firm beneath his touch.

"What did you say?" he asked disinterestedly as his hands roamed on her bare skin.

"I said you . . . play beautifully."

They were both laughing when the knock came at the door. Jessica hurriedly tied the drawstring on her blouse, but Luke put his fingers to her lips, encouraging her to be still and ignore the knock. "Can't be important; besides, I have plans for us before dinner," he whispered, kissing her and holding her close. "And I don't want to be interrupted."

But something told Jessica she should answer the door, a sense of foreboding, a feeling of anxiety. Trying to stay calm, she said lightly, "Maybe we should see who it is. . . ."

"Probably the manager complaining that we've used all the water," he joked as he kissed her again and then reluctantly went to the door.

It was the young bellboy. He spoke in valiant but broken English. "*Señorita* Hale, it is the *teléfono*."

She felt something churn in her stomach and knew her fears had not been misplaced. While Luke tried to explain to the bellboy that there must be a mistake, Jessica slipped on her sandals and wordlessly started down the hall.

"Jessica," he called after her, "no one knows we're here." But even as he spoke, he realized that someone did know.

Silently Luke watched Jessica retreat toward the wide steps that led to the lobby and the hotel's one telephone. Standing at the door, still half-dressed, his chest bare, the look of consternation on his face changed to one of barely restrained anger. He stepped back into the room, and as Jessica reached the lobby she heard the heavy wooden door slam behind him.

She returned a few minutes later, white-faced, the pain evident in her eyes. He didn't notice. He was sitting in a high back wicker chair, his arms crossed, waiting, and he didn't even glance up. "I thought we agreed not to tell anyone we were coming here, Jessica. I thought this was our time together." He looked up then. "Who the hell was calling you?"

Only the onslaught of his words could have pushed from her mind the grave message that had brought the pain. "Luke, I couldn't do it. I had to tell—just one person."

"We made a pact, Jessica," Luke interrupted, more in sorrow than in anger. "What made you . . . *who* made you break it?"

Jessica sank down onto the bed, hands in her lap, feeling very vulnerable. Luke saw that, and his defenses began to melt. He started to move toward her, but then he hesitated, waiting. He wanted an answer. In spite of the vulnerability, in spite of whatever had happened, the answer was one simple word. He wanted her to speak it.

The vulnerability was real. She was like a schoolgirl sitting before him, and she felt no less defenseless than a schoolgirl might have felt. She wanted to fall into his arms and let him comfort her, she wanted to tell him everything, but she held back.

"Jessica," he said softly. "Tell me what's happened."

Jessica looked up at him with hopeful eyes. If he believed in her, he would understand that she couldn't tell him yet. "I have to go back to New Orleans tonight."

She heard him draw a sharp breath.

"I know it's something serious, Jessica," he said quietly. "Tell me. Let me help," he offered.

She couldn't tell. The force of her promise—another promise made just moments before on the phone—was too strong for her to resist its hold. "Luke," she whispered, "I can't explain now. I have to go back, but as soon as this is over—" the words caught in her throat "—I'll explain everything." She suddenly remembered the phone conversation and her eyes filled with tears, which she had to blink back. "Soon, very soon, I'll explain everything."

That wasn't enough for Luke. With hands hooked into the waist of his tight-fitting pants, he paced barefoot up and down the red-tiled floor. "It's Dillon, of course," he spat out. "Only he could cause you to drop everything and run. I'm right, aren't I? It's Dillon."

Wordlessly, she nodded.

The setting sun had flooded into the room through the open balcony doors, and a ray of sunlight caught Luke's glasses and flashed brightly, but no more brightly than his eyes behind the horn-rimmed glasses as he turned on her. The sun, and his anger, blinded her. "What's the matter, Jessica?" he asked hoarsely. "Can't he stand to share you?"

The words were like a slap in her face. "Luke," she protested, "that's so unfair."

"Then tell me why the hell he's calling you."

Confusion, indecision, pain—all of these flickered across Jessica's face and reflected in her eyes. She'd promised Crawford not to tell anyone, not even Luke, why he wanted her back in New Orleans so hurriedly. He'd been vehement in making her give her word. But Luke was equally as insistent that she break it.

Sadly, she shook her head. "I can't win, can I?" Jessica asked the question softly, almost to herself. "If I tell you, then I betray a promise to Crawford, and if I refuse, then you think I don't trust you."

"Promise?" Fiercely he grabbed on to that one word out of all she'd said. "What about your promise to me to tell no one where we were, to keep our time together private?"

Jessica's answer did nothing to calm Luke's ire. "I didn't think he'd call. I didn't think anything so important—"

"More important than us?"

"Of course not." Jessica's voice became sharp with anger now. "But Crawford needs me, and I can't refuse him."

Luke's face was stony. "What is it—some business deal? A giant coup for Modern Times that Dillon can't handle alone?" His words were sarcastic; Luke knew as well as she that Dillon was still the consummate wheeler-dealer.

Jessica nodded. "There is a business deal."

His look was frigid.

"Luke, please," she begged. "There's more." She tried to explain the reason she'd come so close to tears on the phone. "I believe Crawford's ill. If so, he needs me."

"How very convenient," Luke answered. "You happen to leave a number, he happens to call and now he happens to be ill, or so you think. In my opinion, that's what he wants you to think. It's his way of getting you back to New Orleans."

She was angry now, torn between the ties of the past and the strong pull of the present. "I don't have a medical report," she snapped, "but Crawford wouldn't call if he didn't need me. I have to go."

Luke, still standing in the middle of the room, directed white-hot anger at dual targets: the woman who'd so recently shared his bed and the man who had the power to take her away.

"So you go running." He stared across the balcony into the fading light, seeing only what he wanted to see. "You run to the man who controls Jessica Hale. I don't believe he's ill," he said again. "I think he wants to let me—and you—know who's boss."

Stunned by his words, angry at his insinuations about Crawford's motives, Jessica abruptly marched to the closet and pulled out her suitcase. In silence she began to stuff her clothes haphazardly inside. His other words had hurt her; these infuriated her. Abruptly she stopped packing. He'd turned his back, and Jessica had to cross the room to face him. She did, fuming.

"You're behaving just like you did on 'Speak Out,'" she accused. "You're setting yourself up as my prosecutor and my judge."

"For God's sake, Jessica, that's behind us, a part of

the past," Luke said, his voice a whisper of barely controlled rage. "We're talking about now. *Now*, Jessica, when we're two different people." The rage subsided. "We've changed."

"I know we have, Luke," she said softly. "That's why I hoped you'd understand and trust me."

She waited long enough for him to answer, and then she waited a little longer before she walked away with a sigh, pulled the rest of her clothes from the closet and stuffed them into her bag.

"All I know," Luke said finally, "is that an hour ago we were in that bed making love. Now I'm watching you leave."

"Luke. . . . " It was still possible, Jessica believed, to hold on to what they had. "I don't want to leave. You must understand that. This time—our time together here—has been so . . . perfect."

"Then don't spoil it," he said almost tenderly. "Stay here with me. We have two more days. Don't end it now, Jessica." He took a long step forward, across his pain and anger.

But she knew that she had to go; she shook her head.

He nodded silently and a bitter smile crossed his face.

When she saw the smile, she knew all was lost, yet she still tried to erase it with her words. She said softly, "Don't you realize that I'd never leave you if I didn't have to?" *Understand me,* her heart cried out, but there was no answer to the cry.

Luke ran his hands through his dark hair, which had fallen untidily across his forehead. The shirt he'd slipped on hung unbuttoned to his waist, and Jessica could see the rapid rise and fall of his chest. "I won't allow Crawford Dillon to dictate how and when we can be together. You have to choose, Jessica," he ordered. "Dillon or me."

Jessica answered in a strained voice. "This isn't a contest, Luke, and I'm not a prize." She paused and then added the words both of them hated to hear. "I must go back to New Orleans tonight."

Any shimmer of hope she'd held on to was gone when she looked into his black eyes and remembered that he was a tough strong man who'd fought his way to the top, a man who didn't like to be thwarted and refused to lose.

"Go, Jessica," he said, defeated. "I don't know why I thought I could stop you." He crossed to the chest of drawers where he'd left his wallet and the keys to their rented car. He picked up the keys and handed them to her. "You'll need these. Or do you want me to drive you to the plane—and your rendezvous?"

Jessica hated it, the bitterness in his voice, the anger in his face. She saw their relationship drying up before her eyes like a bouquet of summer flowers beneath the unrelenting sun, and she was powerless to stop it. The whole room, both of them, everything that had been bright and gay was now drab and fading. She could almost see a haze wash over them. It had been easy to be angry at Luke when he was a stranger to her, but now the anger was as gray as the colorless room.

Jessica picked up her handbag and reached for her suitcase. "The desk clerk is driving down to Cabo

San Lucas to meet some guests. He can give me a ride. There's a plane sometime around midnight."

Luke shrugged and walked out onto the balcony. No other word was spoken between them, but even as Jessica made her way downstairs, she kept waiting to hear his voice. She heard nothing but the sound of her own footsteps on the tile.

She climbed into the back seat of the car, taking with her a suitcase full of gifts and a heart full of despair. The young clerk noticed both and started the car with only one glance back into the rearview mirror at the *señorita,* whose hair was dark but whose eyes were as blue as the summer sky. Young, but not unwise, he recognized a lover's quarrel and was politely silent during the long drive to Cabo San Lucas.

Before she allowed herself to think about what lay ahead, Jessica's mind lingered on what she'd left behind, the shattered remains of an affair that began with a tender curiosity and developed into a strong and abiding love. There, she'd admitted it. Love. She loved him.

It had grown so fast, her love for him, that it was deep inside her before she could stop it. And now it was lodged there permanently. It had begun the afternoon they'd ridden out to his log cabin. The sight of the place, the realization that he'd built it with his own hands, had planted the first seeds of her love. It had grown and blossomed with each day—and night—they'd shared: the silly disguises in the Quarter, horseback rides through the quickening of spring, quiet evenings when they'd sat alone and talked. And then there'd been Mexico. No matter what happened she would never forget the vacation that had begun so perfectly. Nor would she ever forget the evening that brought it all to an end.

She looked down at the ocean glimmering faintly under the pale light of the rising moon. Palm trees were silhouetted against the radiance of the sea. Paradise. She was leaving paradise hurriedly but not foolishly. There was no question that she was doing what must be done. She only regretted that Luke didn't have the faith to believe that only her deepest concerns about Crawford would have taken her away.

SHE'D LEFT HIM STANDING on the balcony, his back turned, when she closed the door of their room and went down the stairs for the last time. He was still standing there when she reached the car. And while she was thinking about her love for him, he was there. When she looked out to sea and remembered the reason she'd left, that was the moment Luke turned and went back into the bedroom.

The closet door stood open, his clothes hanging on one side, the other bare. He started to close the door and shut off the memory of her when he saw the nightgown hanging on a peg at the end of the closet. She'd forgotten it. He reached out before he could stop himself and took the flimsy garment in his hands and lifted it from the peg. It was wondrously soft and he remembered the touch of her skin beneath it, and he remembered each time he'd taken it off. He held the gown up to his face. It still had her scent, and the sudden memory of her as he crushed the garment between his hands and buried his face in it brought tears to Luke's eyes. Infuriated with himself, he threw it aside and slammed the closet door.

He wanted to slam doors, throw things, let his rage explode. He thought of picking up the water pitcher by the bed and hurling it into the mirror to watch with grim pleasure as the pieces shattered like the shards of this broken day. But he didn't throw anything.

Instead he automatically began to button his shirt and look for his shoes, but his mind was far from the activities that busied his hands. It was on Jessica, and nothing he could do would tear it away from the thought of her. He tried to replace poignant memories with anger and direct that anger at himself for letting her affect him. He should have never gotten so close, Luke told himself, trying to hold on to the anger. But it started to slip away, and he let it go.

He'd known many women, but none of them had affected him quite like Jessica Hale. She was beautiful beyond reason and bright beyond belief. She was hard to define, guarded yet blatantly truthful. She reminded him of the outdoors and all the things he loved most. Her body, which she barely concealed behind extravagant clothes, made him ache for her just as much when she wore jeans and a man's shirt. He'd never known a more beautiful woman, and he knew no one—man or woman—with her kind of rich probing intelligence. She was determined, ambitious, stubborn—and she was gone.

He cursed softly to himself, picked up his key and left the room. He wouldn't let her absence cause him to throw things, and he wouldn't let it turn him into a morose hermit. He was on vacation, and there were two days left. He'd stay here and enjoy himself, starting tonight. Wearing his resolve like an added piece of clothing he walked downstairs and out into the night.

"LA SENORITA NO ESTA AQUI?" The young waiter stood expectantly at the cantina door looking into the darkness past Luke, waiting for the beautiful *señorita* to materialize.

"No está aquí," Luke parroted back as he headed, not for his usual table, but for the bar. He climbed onto the wicker stool and noticed there were only two other customers, an Englishman and his wife, regulars like Luke and Jessica had been. He read the questions in their faces and turned away. They'd never seen him without her.

He hadn't been without her, not from the time her cab had pulled up next to the old Volkswagen on the deserted stretch of road. They'd eaten together and slept together; they'd watched the sunsets and the sunrises; talked into the night; made love and waked to the sound of church bells in the village; taken long runs on the beach in the early morning and run from the heat at high noon—and everywhere they'd been, they'd been together. Now a part of him was missing.

He called the bartender and defiantly ordered a shot of tequila. As the drink was set before him, Luke was reminded of the first night he and Jessica observed the ritual, taking the obligatory lick of salt before they downed the tequila in one gulp then sucked on a slice of lime and, laughing, choking, vowed they'd never do it again, only to be challenged by the bartender until they gave in and began each evening at the cantina with tequila and laughter.

He didn't need to be in here, Luke thought, with all these memories. He considered going somewhere else, started to get up, changed his mind and ordered another drink.

"*Señor*, you are not eating tonight?" the owner asked. The American had been at the bar for many hours now, not drinking so much but just sitting and staring into space.

"Not tonight," Luke answered.

"The *señorita*. . .she is ill?" Miguel missed her, too. He'd always served one dish *muy picante*—hot and spicy—adding the chili peppers that she agreed to try, pleased with her adventurousness. And Jessica always rewarded him with a smile that beautifully concealed the burning in her throat and waited politely until he walked away to reach for a glass of ice water.

"No, not ill," Luke replied. "The *señorita* has gone away."

Curiosity fought with politeness on Miguel's round face. The Americanos had seemed so happy, *muy contento*, he'd told his wife, who rarely left her stool at the kitchen counter where she pounded out the flour tortillas and supervised the cooking. Several times an evening Miguel took the news of the cantina in to her. Now he'd have to tell his wife that the *señor* was drinking tequila instead of eating dinner and that the *señorita* had gone. Miguel shook his head and made his way through the now-crowded bar toward the kitchen.

Still later in the evening, Luke wasn't sure what time, he found himself sitting in a chair at a deserted table, holding Pedro's guitar. Lightly he struck a chord. It was a mournful sound, the antithesis of the music he'd drawn from the same instrument only the night before. That had been an upbeat rhythm, eliciting cheers and laughter. This was a plaintive sound that caused those who remained at this late hour to look up in wonder at the sadness of the music.

Luke played on, unmindful of his audience. With each sad strum of the guitar he thought of Jessica. He remembered the first time he saw her, anger building in her vibrant body, sparks in her surprisingly blue eyes, defiance in the tilt of her dark head. He knew then he'd never seen a woman like her. And he was right. His mind traveled back to the beginning, the real beginning for them. She was in the woods beside the river, handling the horse with ease, dressed in jeans and the tight shirt that stretched provocatively across her breasts. He remembered her eyes widening with disbelief and wonder when he showed her the cabin. There were other images, too. Jessica making love, her dark hair on the pillow, her lush body opening to him. She had so many moods, so many colors and shades of emotion. Luke had never forgotten the tenderness he'd felt when she admitted that she wrote poetry, and then the laughter they'd shared over the complexity of her lines. She'd laid her heart bare to him.

With a final discordant note his fingers raked

across the strings, and he put the guitar aside. After dropping a handful of bills on the table, he waved his thanks to Pedro and stalked into the night.

The music and the memories had made clear to Luke what he'd long known. He was in love with her. That's why the hurt of her leaving had turned to anger, causing him to lash out against Dillon. Luke knew there was nothing romantic about Jessica and her mentor, but still he was jealous, jealous that Dillon had the power to tear them apart. His feelings might be irrational, but they were real and very painful.

Luke stuffed his hands deep into his pants pockets and carefully navigated the path down to the inn. He could feel the beginning of a headache; he'd have a tequila hangover the next day as powerful as the Mexican sunrise. But the pounding in his head was nothing compared to the compelling emotion that overtook him. The woman he loved was tied to another man with bonds as long as a lifetime and as strong as loyalty itself.

Abruptly he stopped, bathed in moonlight, his head raised toward the stars. He wouldn't be shut out of the private world Jessica and Crawford shared. Luke Maxwell was a man who'd fought all his life for what he wanted no matter the odds. He'd wanted an education; he'd gotten it. He'd wanted an academic position; he'd gotten it. He'd wanted to influence people's thinking on subjects that mattered in the world. He'd gotten that, too. He wanted a career in politics, and even that seemed within reach. Nothing had been denied him. Until now. He wasn't going to give up. He'd break the ties that bound Jessica to Crawford Dillon. Strong as they were, his love for Jessica was stronger.

Luke straightened his shoulders and continued along the path. Mexico and Santa Isabella had lost their charm. He wanted no more of them. He'd get on the first available flight out of Cabo San Lucas and be with Jessica tomorrow night. They'd talk it all out, argue and fight—and resolve it. Luke was filled with purpose and determination. He was a man in love. Nothing could stop him now.

7

TWO PEOPLE IN DIFFERENT PARTS of the city were surprised by Luke Maxwell the following day. The first was Toni Allen.

Toni was the perfect mixture of business acumen and personal savvy. When Jessica had called the office asking her to have files available immediately, Toni had known something important was about to happen. The files included Jessica's personal research on the upcoming merger with New Look health spas as well as depositions and recommendations from the boards of directors of both companies. Big things were brewing.

Toni was familiar with the details of the proposed takeover, and now that the time of finalization was near, she knew that both companies—because of the reaction over stock transfers—wanted everything under wraps until the announcement was made. Jessica's return from her vacation two days early meant the time was now. Toni's business sense told her that; her instincts told her more. Jessica was upset. Toni heard it in her voice, and when Jessica stopped to pick up the files, she saw it in her face. Something more was going on at the Crawford Dillon estate than the discussion of the New Look plans, and whatever it was, it was serious.

She wasn't the only one who suspected something was in the wind. The phone had been ringing all day. Toni was beginning to be able to anticipate who the next caller would be each time it rang, but Luke Maxwell was a surprise. She paused when she heard the voice. He identified himself, although it wasn't necessary. She'd recognize that voice anywhere. She paused for a second to let a mental picture of him flit by. Good-looking. Sexy. And unfortunately her boss's nemesis. She assumed he was calling about a possible follow-up interview, and unless Jessica's feelings about his show had changed drastically, Toni knew what the answer would be. She decided to let him talk anyway; the voice was worth listening to.

"I'm sorry, Miss Hale isn't in," she said politely.

"When do you expect her?" The voice was curt, but Toni had sweetened harsher callers than this one.

"Miss Hale is working out of the office today, but—"

"Where?" Luke asked without even an attempt at civility.

Toni, a little irritated now, was still determined to see this conversation through. "I'm not sure that—"

"She didn't leave a number where she could be reached?" The voice was incredulous; Toni knew that she hadn't fooled him, but she let the game go on even without his participation.

"No, but she'll be calling in, I'm sure. I'll leave a

message for her." She decided to hang on a little longer to see if she could warm the cold voice on the other end. "Or if you'd like to tell me what the call refers to, I'll relay the message to Miss Hale—or maybe I could help you myself."

"No, thanks." The phone went dead.

Toni put down the receiver and shook her head. Something was on that man's mind, and it was puzzling. It had been a strange day all around. She didn't know then how much stranger it was going to get. She began to have an idea when the phone rang the next time.

"It's Luke Maxwell, again," he said, somewhat more friendly. "I'm concerned about Miss Hale."

Now, that *was* puzzling, Toni thought.

"She left Mexico rather unexpectedly—"

Toni let out an audible gasp and then coughed to cover it while Luke continued.

"I wanted to make sure that she arrived safely and that everything was all right."

"Yes," Toni said meaninglessly. "Er, that is, she did return and she is all right." Finally she could stand the suspense no longer. "You were with her—in Mexico?"

"That's right."

"Oh." Toni's eyebrows arched. She stretched her long legs out, crossed them and leaned back in her chair, smiling. What a day. "Well," she said then.

"I know you can understand why I'm so anxious to get in touch with her," he continued.

"Yes." Toni realized that her last few monosyllables had not been exactly brilliant, but she was stunned. She tried to recover.

"I have reason to believe that she's meeting with Mr. Dillon," Maxwell said, a little speculatively, Toni thought. "Maybe you'd be good enough to give me his unlisted number. . . ."

"Oh, no." Toni sat up straight and tried to open the business niche of her mind, which she'd left closed for a moment.

"Toni, I was with her in Mexico—"

"Actually, I don't know that for a fact."

"How else would I have known where she went or when she came back?" Luke tried to control the irritation in his voice.

"You could have seen her at the airport. Lots of reporters—"

"Toni," Luke said slyly, "she was wearing a wig."

"No! Really? Good Lord, I love it!" Toni's mouth curved into a delighted smile.

"Somehow, I thought you would. Now can I have the number?"

"I'm taking a terrible chance doing this, but you know something? I'm not concerned."

"You have no reason to be," Luke responded, noting the number, thanking her and hanging up.

THE BUTLER WHO ANSWERED THE PHONE at Fortune's Rest knew every voice, every name, every face that was important to Crawford Dillon. He didn't recognize the voice of Luke Maxwell. Since he wasn't a television fan, he didn't even recognize the name.

"I'm sorry," he said politely but adamantly. "Miss Hale is unable to come to the phone."

"Then let me speak to Mr. Dillon," Luke insisted.

"Mr. Dillon is not available, either." The butler could hear the mumbled curse at the other end of the line. It didn't faze him; he was used to such behavior when he had to screen callers.

"Then will you take a message for Miss Hale?"

"Certainly, sir." He neglected to tell the caller that both Miss Hale and Mr. Dillon had left an hour before.

The butler took the name, home number and office number carefully, paying no attention to the barely concealed anger in the caller's voice.

"Tell her it's urgent."

"Of course, sir." The line went dead.

ARCH WHEELER WAS SURPRISED, not by a phone call but by an open door when he passed Luke's office on his way home that evening. Every schedule at the station had been rearranged so that Luke could get away for a week, and here he was back two days early. Arch Wheeler was not only surprised; he was irritated. The former showed; the latter did not. He was a careful man. Only once in his career had he allowed himself to lose his temper, years earlier with his partner, Crawford Dillon. He'd been a young man then, and very trusting. That was the first—and last—professional problem he'd been unable to handle. Since that day he'd called all the shots, based on his very high standards and, some said, his impossibly strict morality. He didn't put up with bad judgments, poor choices or even bad planning. It seemed to him that Luke had not planned well, and he wanted to know why.

Wheeler stood in the doorway for a moment, lit his pipe and surveyed the situation. Luke was sitting at his desk, the phone inches away, and although there was work piled up, he didn't appear to have made a swipe at it. Wheeler walked in and sat down. "Explanation, please." Under these circumstances, he could be a man of few words.

The brusqueness didn't bother Luke; he'd heard it before, and he'd always handled it in the easiest possible way—by being honest. He often handled it in equally few words, as today.

"Interrupted love affair" was his explanation.

"I can understand that. Women are unpredictable." Wheeler had never married, probably for that very reason. "Judging by your proximity to the phone after working hours, I would gather 'thirty' hasn't yet been written on this story," he said, using the newspaper term for "the end."

"That's my hope," Luke responded. There was a long pause, and when his boss didn't ask, he volunteered the rest. "Her name's Jessica Hale."

"Modern Times?"

Luke nodded.

"Steer clear of her," Wheeler said.

Luke had expected Wheeler's reaction about the unnecessary rescheduling, but he hadn't expected any reaction at all to Jessica's name, particularly not this one. "Why?" he asked, startled.

Wheeler shifted his pipe to one side of his mouth

and pushed his sleeves up a little farther. They were already rolled high, his collar loosened and a pencil jammed behind his ear, all in the tradition of the old-time newspaper reporter. The world of television hadn't changed Wheeler's philosophy or his mannerisms; it certainly hadn't changed his image. He was a hard man, and it showed in his square stocky frame on which there wasn't an extra ounce of fat. It showed in his dealings with people, in the way he played tennis—still a tough opponent at fifty-six—and it showed most dramatically in his professional life. He was proud of that. Wheeler didn't want to see his protégé fall into a trap, and anyone in close proximity to Crawford Dillon was not to be trusted, in Wheeler's opinion.

"My objections to her employer go way back." He saw from Luke's expression that was not news. "You know about our past relationship?" he asked.

"Only that it existed. Jessica told me nothing more."

Wheeler told him the rest. "We were in business together years ago, and we came to a parting of ways over some very important issues." He paused to frame his next words. "They are fundamental, and they still exist."

"They don't involve Jessica," Luke replied adamantly.

"Of course not," Wheeler conceded, "but she seems to be inextricably tied to Dillon and hence his values, which have not changed, in my opinion. His is a pleasure-principle philosophy." He saw that Luke wanted to interrupt, but he was determined to say the rest. "Your reputation is spotless, and so is your background. Just be careful."

Luke smiled. "Dillon and Jessica are two different people, Arch."

Wheeler nodded, admitting the truth of Luke's words, but unwilling to concede that there wasn't a reason to be wary. "Oh, I never thought that Dillon's hold on the girl was sexual, but there are other ties, just as strong. Be careful that in pursuing her you don't get Crawford Dillon, too. That would be a questionable pair for you to carry into the political arena."

"Well, I'm not in politics yet; besides, I'm not exactly carrying Jessica anywhere. She hasn't even returned my calls."

"Then maybe we should go to dinner and finish this conversation," Wheeler said. "I had something else I wanted to talk to you about when you got back, and since you're back.... Let's see if we can beat the crowd at Stephen and Martin's; I've been craving those oysters." They got up to go. "Funny," he said, "how a man can never outgrow or escape the past." Luke could not know then how prophetic those words were.

JESSICA STOOD LOOKING OUT of the hospital room window hardly seeing the bright glow of morning sun. Behind her the bed was freshly made, the sheets stretched tightly, a light blanket folded at the foot. There was a glass of water on the night table and several vases of flowers were placed around the room. More would be arriving, she knew, now that the news had hit the papers. She hadn't looked at them yet, but they were waiting, stacked next to the visitor's chair. She finally turned from the window to pick up the paper on top. It was on the front page, a photograph of her and Dillon getting out of the car in front of the hospital the previous afternoon.

The article was sketchy because the facts had not been available. It stated only that Dillon, accompanied by his business associate, Jessica Hale, had checked into the hospital for tests and that his condition was thought to be serious.

It *was* serious. Jessica tossed the paper aside and collapsed into the chair. She hadn't slept all night, sitting beside Crawford's bed, unable to rid herself of the possibility that the prognosis would be negative. All indications pointed to the failure of an artificial heart valve that had been inserted several years before. This morning's battery of tests would indicate whether surgery to replace the valve would be possible. Even those vital tests had been put off until the last moment with meetings at Crawford's house culminating in the final signing of the merger while a car waited outside to take him to the hospital.

The morning hours crept toward noon with the arrival of more flowers and messages. Some of the calls were important and would have to be handled, but not now, not until she found out what was going to happen to the man who had for so many years been the center of her life.

Another hour passed before the doctor appeared at the door. "It's what we suspected, Jessica," he said seriously. "The tube is not functioning properly. I'd hoped we could find another problem that would be more easily remedied, but. . . ."

Jessica felt the tears sting her eyes. "What did the tests show?" she asked softly.

"That's the good part, Jessica. Crawford is very strong. All of his other signs are good. His red corpuscle count is normal. I'm confident that he'll come through open-heart surgery easily. Once the valve is replaced and functioning, he'll be as good as new."

"Thank God," Jessica said as she sank back in the chair. "Will he be coming up now?"

The doctor shook his head. "He'll be down in X-ray for another hour or two."

"I'll stay until he comes back to the room," Jessica said, and the doctor nodded. He knew that Jessica's devotion was important to his patient.

"Crawford did ask that you handle the messages and do one more favor—call out to Fortune's Rest for his burgundy-red pajamas and robe. Apparently he plans to do some entertaining before the surgery. Claims he won't be seen in a tacky hospital gown. He also asked for a pitcher of mint juleps, but I declined that one."

For the first time in almost two days, Jessica smiled—a wide-open smile, not one of the forced curves she'd attempted for Crawford's benefit. "I'll do that right away, and then I'll get to these messages." She picked up the stack of previously ignored phone calls. "I'm sure some of them are business—" She stopped in midsentence, and when the doctor asked her if anything was wrong, she answered with a monosyllable and another smile. Nothing was wrong. Half the messages were from Luke!

The doctor had barely gotten out the door when a nurse, matronly and round, bustled in, bringing the news that she'd barely been able to contain during the long walk down the hall. "There's a call at the nurse's station, Miss Hale. It's . . . it's . . . ."

"I can't take any calls now," Jessica said firmly. It could be important, but there was one more important call she had to make first. "Ask the switchboard to continue taking messages and have them sent to Mr. Dillon's room."

"But this one's for *you,*" the nurse answered. "He said he already left eight messages so he called the nurse's station direct. Don't know how he got that number."

Jessica had already started for the door. Only one person could charm his way past the switchboard right to the surgery floor. Mrs. Perkins, still talking, ran along beside, her short stout legs doing double-time to keep up.

"I wouldn't have bothered you, Miss Hale, but it's Luke Maxwell! Well, I just knew it must be important, not just the normal inquiry. He's so. . . . I watch his show whenever I can. He's so . . . ."

Jessica just smiled. By the time she reached for the phone, not only Mrs. Perkins but every nurse at the station was avidly and openly listening. Jessica tried not to show the emotion she felt as she said his name. It wasn't easy.

"Luke."

"Have I had a time finding you," he said, and she

let his voice wrap warmly around her, and all the strain began to leave her tired body.

"I've been here all night, I—"

"How is he?" Luke's voice was concerned.

"He'll have to have surgery, but he's going to be okay, I'm sure of that now after talking to the doctor."

"I want to see you, Jessica. I need to see you." Luke's voice was vibrant with urgency.

"I'll be here a couple more hours. Maybe we could meet someplace. If it wasn't for the press. . . ."

"I mean now, Jessica." He was adamant.

"Luke, there're reporters all over the hospital lobby. You can't—"

"I'm already at the hospital. I'm downstairs."

"Luke, how did you get by the press?" Jessica found herself smiling. When Luke Maxwell decided to do something a whole contingent of reporters couldn't stop him.

"Never mind, I was tired of calling and leaving messages so I decided to come to you. What floor are you on?"

"Six, but—"

"I'll come up the back stairs. Is there a waiting room at the north corner of the building?"

"Yes, there's a small one just for this wing. It's not private but there's no press." Jessica could see the door to the waiting room from where she stood. The stairs were right around the corner. That would be easier, she decided, than having Luke try to make it to Crawford's room through the defensive line of nurses.

"I'll be there in two minutes."

Jessica hung up, tried to ignore the open-mouthed stares of the still-growing group of nurses, turned and walked casually toward the end of the hall. To her surprise, no one followed, but there were several people seated in the waiting room. While they obviously recognized Jessica, they were quiet, lost in the self absorption that comes with long hours of vigil. But when Luke Maxwell appeared, the whole atmosphere seemed to change; he brought an air of vitality with him that dispelled the anxiety. A murmur of excitement spread around the room. Jessica heard that before she saw Luke.

For an instant it looked as if she might hurl herself into his arms. She knew that if she did, everyone in the room would approve, but her own sense of privacy and decorum in this solemn place restrained her. She stood up and held out her hand instead, but she was trembling.

"I'm glad you're here," she said. "Oh, Luke, I knew he was ill."

"I realize that now, Jessica." Luke sat down beside her on the little plastic sofa. She had removed her hand from his grasp, and they remained a few inches apart, touching only with their eyes. "You look so tired," he said, and there was an ache for her in his voice. "Tell me about it," he probed gently.

"It's a heart valve. I called the doctor when I got back from Mexico, even before calling Crawford. He'd apparently been tired and short of breath for some time, but he didn't mention that to me, of course, or to anyone. By last week the symptoms had intensified, and yesterday he finally agreed to check into the hospital. The tests today showed that he needs open-heart surgery, but he's a prime candidate for it because of his excellent physical condition." Jessica knew Luke could feel her relief. He reached across the small space that separated them and touched her hand. "He'll need medication and a proper diet for a few days before the surgery—for extra insurance. Then he'll come through with flying colors, I'm sure," she finished in a breathless whisper. Luke didn't take his eyes from hers nor his hand from her hand. He waited.

"Luke. . . ." She wanted to say more, about them, about why she left, about how she felt this moment with him beside her.

"If I could just hold you. . . ." He looked around and then pulled her up suddenly and led her across the room and out onto the balcony with all eyes watching. It was a narrow concrete-and-steel structure, coldly unappealing, but it was just what he wanted, for in the far corner they were out of view of the waiting room. With a sigh of relief and release, they fell into each other's arms.

"Jessica, oh Jessica," he murmured. "I'm so sorry for not trusting you." He buried his face in her hair and wrapped his arms around her.

Mutely, she nodded. She wanted nothing more than to feel the strength of his body and its comforting warmth. When she spoke it was a denial. "No," she said, "I should apologize." She leaned back in his arms, searching his face. "I promised not to tell anyone where we were, Luke, and I broke that promise.

But something—some instinct—told me to give Crawford the number. I knew he'd never call unless there was an emergency."

"And there was," he said.

"Yes. Oh, Luke," she cried, "I didn't know how ill he was, but I knew he'd never call unless it was serious. And he was determined to finalize that damn business deal. I had to be with him."

Luke nodded. "That's why he didn't check into the hospital until yesterday afternoon."

"Yes," Jessica said. "He took a real risk, but I couldn't do anything to stop him. He insisted I keep it quiet until the papers were signed." She sighed deeply. "Oh, Luke, I felt so torn between the two of you. Crawford's been my whole world for so many years, but I'm a big girl now. There's someone else in my life." She touched his cheek lovingly. "And what did I do just when I realized that?" She answered her own question. "I left you there in Mexico and ran off. Never, never again, Luke."

"Wait a minute," he interjected. "I get some of the blame. I was too busy being jealous and insecure to realize something serious was happening."

She looked at him, her eyes wide and solemn. "If Crawford makes it through surgery—and I know he will—I'm going to do two things."

"Namely?" He gave her a quizzical smile.

"I'm going to have a personal life at long last."

"With a vengeance, I hope," he said, kissing the corner of her mouth. "And what else?"

"I'm going to get rid of that centerfold," she vowed fervently.

They rocked in laughter, holding on to each other and releasing all the pent-up tension that had come between them over the past two agonizing days with their parting and Crawford's illness. Jessica had been like a spring, wound up and ready to snap. Now, in Luke's arms, she felt the tension flow from her body.

"I'm sorry for leaving you like that," she repeated.

"And I'm sorry for not understanding," he replied. "Just remember, next time tell me what's going on. I don't ever want to read about it in the paper again!"

IT WAS MIDAFTERNOON WHEN JESSICA got to her office, and Toni was there to greet her. She'd heard Crawford's prognosis, so Toni's relief allowed her an opening for the question she'd been toying with since the day before. She extended her long body across the doorway as Jessica approached, the signal that an interesting remark was forthcoming. It turned out to be more interesting than Jessica might have expected.

"What's this about Luke Maxwell and you in Mexico?"

Jessica stopped in her tracks, looked sharply at Toni, ducked under her arm and went into the office. "How in the world did you know?" she called out over her shoulder as she headed for the desk.

"He phoned here looking for you. Sounded kinda wild. Told me he had to find you. I gave him your number at Crawford's—"

"Against all orders," Jessica reminded her as she sat down behind the overflowing desk.

"But not against my better judgment. Besides, you'd already left for the hospital by then," Toni said, "according to the papers."

"Yes, Crawford checked in yesterday afternoon."

"Did Luke find you?" Toni was obviously determined to pursue the matter right to the end.

"You're awfully nosy," Jessica teased.

Toni put her hands on her slim hips, tilted her head and gave Jessica a reproving look. "That beautiful sexy bundle of man tells me you've been in Mexico together, and you're playing coy?"

Jessica laughed. "No, I'm not playing coy. We did go away together and it was wonderful—while it lasted."

"While it lasted? You mean it's over?" Toni looked at Jessica as if she'd just been told her boss was planning to take up residence on the moon.

"I'm seeing him tonight. Does that satisfy you?"

Toni flashed her brightest smile. "Perfectly."

"Just remember that we're keeping this. . .friendship. . .quiet. I don't want to be in the papers again—at least for another week."

"Now, Jessica—" Toni said as she straightened up to leave the doorway "—all your secrets are safe with me."

THE LAST TWO HOURS of the working day were crowded with a review of all the department heads' activities while she'd been gone. At six o'clock, with the major fires put out, the Chicago and L.A. offices appeased, the stock merger news digested and, finally, with the latest news about Crawford positive, Jessica could draw a deep breath. That's when Monty LaBaux sauntered into her office.

She'd meant to squeeze in a meeting with him earlier about *Scope* deadlines but had put it off because he'd always been able to handle his own problems. This time was no exception. It was still light outside when, fifteen minutes later, all their business was taken care of.

Monty still looked fresh and debonair as he closed his files, not daunted by the heat or the pressures of his job. He checked the slim gold watch on his wrist, threw a glance at Jessica's well-organized desk and said with a pointed air of admiration, "Cleaned everything up, have you? And now you're ready to go," he observed. "Not that I expected an early evening tête-à-tête in the boss's office, but do you have to sit on the edge of your chair, Jessica? I know when my time is up."

Jessica started to object and tried to settle back as if she had all night. Neither attempt was successful.

Monty smiled his perfect white smile and shook his head. "Smacks of infatuation to me."

She tried again, this time to look puzzled, realized she'd failed miserably and gave up. "You're certainly observant, Monty."

He made a gesture of acceptance. "One of the tools of my trade. So don't disappoint me and say I'm wrong."

"I just want to get home, actually. It's been a long day."

"Get home to . . .? Come on, Jessica, I see a male reflection in those gorgeous eyes and regret to say the image is not me." When she didn't answer, he flashed another smile, shrugged, adjusted the already perfect knot in his tie and got to his feet. "Okay, boss. Let's call it a day."

"Are you sure we've covered everything?"

"Ah, I detect a note of guilt. Yes, dear Jessica, anything else can wait." Monty turned to go and then remembered the file folder he'd set aside for last but subsequently forgotten in his fascination with what was buzzing through Jessica's startling mind. "There is one more thing. You'll find it interesting, I believe—the rough draft of that article Sharon Jessup's been working on."

At Jessica's blank look, he reminded her. "You asked to see the draft, remember? Jessica, I do believe you've forgotten." He held up the file. "This is the Maxwell story Sharon dug so hard for." He grinned and tossed the folder on her desk. "I think you'll find it fascinating, but not tonight," he said with another grin. "We'll discuss it in the morning. See you then," he said as he closed the door behind him.

Jessica let the folder lie untouched. Monty was right. She'd forgotten about the assignment made that April day in the heat of anger. It had all happened long ago—before her life and Luke's had become so unexpectedly intertwined. She would never let *Scope* run the story on him now. To profile her lover in a Modern Times magazine reeked of unprofessionalism. No, Sharon Jessup's final draft would never be written. Jessica wasn't about to use her relationship with Luke, still in the formative, even fragile stages, to boost the sales of *Scope*. As for any thought of revenge, that had long ago fled from her mind on the strong wings of her love.

She stood up, ready to leave. Then she sat back down, drawn like a magnet to that tempting folder. Her curiosity was getting the better of her, and she knew she'd have to look.

It was as she had expected. Nothing new. She flipped through the pages quickly. The research was certainly complete with everything there—his childhood, the boyhood years of struggling, the jobs to pay for his education. There was a list of part-time jobs he'd held, a few he hadn't told Jessica about—house painter, truck driver, salesman. Evidently he'd taken any job in his pursuit of an education. She thought about her own background; she'd experienced none of Luke's deprivation, while he'd worked all of his life to make something of himself. That was one of the reasons she cared about him. Luke was a man she could respect, as well as love. If there was nothing unexpected in the article, it served to remind her of how she felt about this man.

She closed the cover of the file and was putting it in her briefcase when she noticed the handwritten notation: *see photos of Maxwell modeling job*. Jessica thumbed through the background information in the file, looking for the photos. She wasn't surprised that Luke had worked as a model; he was certainly handsome enough in an all-American kind of way and his body.... Jessica smiled in remembrance. He had a great body.

The photographs were in a magazine, its cover clipped back to the full-color spread. Jessica let out a little gasp. There were half a dozen pictures, fascinating, no, astounding, made when he was in his twenties, she judged, young, handsome—and stark raving naked!

Jessica's eyes were riveted to Luke's long sleek limbs, strong chest, broad shoulders. There was more than just the way he looked; there was the way she *felt*. A blatant sexuality emanated from the pages, and Jessica could feel her emotions begin to churn. The poses were provocative while they were artistic. And sexy. Definitely very sexy. The photographer had shot Luke not against an exotic background but very simply against a white backdrop.

Jessica leaned back in her chair and grinned. Well, well. Luke Maxwell still had some secrets he hadn't shared with her. She couldn't wait to tease him about his career as a nude model. He'd be embarrassed, she suspected, or maybe not. Luke was anything but predictable. Whatever his reaction, it was very exciting to discover this thoroughly delicious side of him.

She removed the clip on the magazine cover. It was a slick-looking publication that had enjoyed brief popularity then vanished from the newsstands.

What had possessed him, she wondered, to allow his picture in this kind of magazine? Jessica checked the date on the cover. Obviously it was a time when Luke had been especially hard up for money.

She slipped the magazine back into the folder and put it in her briefcase. Luke was probably at her house waiting for her. She'd lingered longer than she meant to over the photographs. Tonight would be quite a night. Besides the talking and making up, there was this little bombshell to drop. As Jessica waited for the elevator, the image of a nude Luke lingered in her mind and stayed with her through the drive home.

8

IT WAS A DRIVE that took twice as long as usual, because in her rush Jessica managed to miss every light, and then she had to wait at St. Charles while the trolley disgorged its passengers with agonizing slowness before it methodically clanked and rattled on. She reached her turn at last and sped down the wide shaded street. The glossy leaves of the live oaks and magnolias shimmered in the heat that had accumulated through a long sunny June day. In each shimmering leaf she saw visions of Luke, all provocative, all sexy—all nude. By the time she got to her house, Jessica was beginning to feel a little ashamed of her downright lascivious feelings about her lover. She turned into her driveway literally blushing at herself and then felt even more absurd because his car wasn't behind the garage where he usually parked.

"Damn," she said aloud, remembering all of her beautiful wasted thoughts. She wondered why he hadn't come and then supposed he had come and gone, impatient at her lateness. Well, she'd call and tell him just what she'd been doing to make her so late! Jessica let herself in the back door and headed for the kitchen phone.

She saw him out of the corner of her eye. He was standing in the living room, leaning against the mantel and looking wonderfully cool in the glimmering sunlight that streamed through the windows. He grinned and answered her unasked question.

"Parked the car a couple of blocks away and then stole surreptitiously down side streets and through backyards to the kitchen door. I was sure glad to find my key still hidden under the flowerpot, because you're even later than usual, Jessica," he said, glancing at his watch. "I helped myself to a drink—"

Jessica didn't wait for him to finish. She dropped her briefcase and handbag at her feet and rushed toward him, happy to see him and relieved there were no eyes watching them this time. She took his face in her hands and looked up at him. "I can't think of a nicer way to end the day. I was afraid you'd gotten impatient and left."

"Read every book in your library," he said, hugging her close. "But I'm not complaining—now that you're here. Hmm," he added, feeling her warm and eager against him. "You really *are* here."

"You bet I am! And there's nowhere I'd rather be at the end of a long hot day."

"I'll bet you say that to all your men."

"No." She looked up at him. "Only the ones with deep brown eyes and thick hair and a beautiful mouth and a wonderful body and—"

"Maybe we should fight more often," he said huskily, "if this is how we make up."

"Are we making up?" Jessica asked in wide-eyed

innocence before kissing him longingly and thoroughly.

"No," he mumbled through the kisses.

"No?" She drew back a little in mock surprise.

"We already made up at the hospital. What we're doing now is making *love*. There's a difference." His kiss told her what he meant. It was a kiss probing and caring, just like the one at the hospital, but there was no restraint in it, no holding back. This kiss would lead them far beyond the other. Yet the hospital still loomed in the background, and Luke knew that it still occupied a corner of Jessica's mind. He asked her about it so that she could explain and then put it away from her for now.

"How is Crawford?"

"Doing well and actually looking forward to the surgery," she answered, still holding on tightly. "It's a relief for Crawford to know that the problem can be repaired. He was very relaxed when I left him."

"Now it's your turn to relax."

"Yes," she mumbled against his chest.

"That's what I'm here for." He ran his hands up her back from the curving hollow below her waist to the nape of her neck. "Silk again," he mumbled, caressing her through the soft blouse. "Always silk. Even in bed. By the way," he added, "you left your nightgown in Mexico."

"Did I?" she asked, uninterested.

"I'll give it back on one condition."

"What's that?" she asked, hardly caring as he nibbled at her ear, his breath sending shivers of anticipation through her.

"That you leave it in the closet when I'm here. It's nice, Jessica. But you're nicer. It's soft, delicate and sexy, but you—" his lips slid across her face and captured her mouth again "—you give me ideas."

"I think I like your ideas," Jessica managed to whisper as her body registered his physical presence from the front of his shirt against her thrusting breasts to the lightweight trousers covering his lean hard thighs. She could feel the buckle on his belt pressing against her, the day's growth of beard tickling her face, the strong hands pressing into her back. She could even feel the edge of his hipbone, but the overpowering sensation—greater than the scent of his cologne, the taste of his lips—was the growing strength of his manhood throbbing there, just where her own desire centered. It filled her mind, took over her body and brought back the flashing images of him in the photographs. He was hers, all of this strong and gentle man was hers. She opened her lips to tell him, but the words didn't come, for his replaced them.

"I want you, Jessica," she heard his voice say what she had wanted to say, those thoughts that had been coursing through her blood like liquid fire, and the smile that lit her face at that voice gave a radiant answering glow. Jessica took Luke's hand and let him lead her up the narrow stairs to her bedroom. The sun was low in the sky, and in its soft glow they undressed, letting their clothes drop unheeded around their feet, kicking away the constricting garments and reaching hungrily for each other.

She felt Luke's skin with all her senses. It was cool

beneath her fingers, cool and hard and very, very real. Jessica traced the line of his collarbone and ran her fingers up the strong column of his neck to tangle in his thick hair. Through it all she felt so small and fragile in his arms, and just as she'd let her body discover him, she felt his eyes discover this: her dark brown hair like a cloud around her shoulders, her blue eyes huge in her face, her lips parted as if waiting for his kiss.

He caressed with his eyes the contrast in the creamy-white and golden-brown of her skin, the outline of her bikini perfectly delineated from the long hours they'd shared in the Mexican sun, and just when he seemed to have seen enough, he took off his glasses and together they walked to the bed.

Jessica leaned back on the fresh clean sheets and he lay down beside her, resting on one elbow, and the kiss came then, soft and gentle, barely grazing her lips, making her ache for more. He was all of those images that had so persistently flashed before her mind, all of them and more, for now the Luke of the pictures was here beside her, flesh and blood, real and loving, as at last he covered her mouth with a kiss that was more than a kiss, that shook her to her very depths.

When he took his mouth from hers, it was only to trace with his tongue the delicate white skin of her breasts. Jessica began to melt in hot desire, closed her eyes and let herself sink as if into a warm buoyant pool. Her whole body softened and flowed toward her lover.

Luke continued to play with her breasts, using his

tongue and lips to tease their eager orbs while Jessica ran her hands across his back, her nails lightly marking the smooth taut muscles that rippled beneath his dark skin. But there was more, for as his mouth worked its magic on her tender swollen breasts, his loving fingers found the soft sweetness of her passion's center, and she was swept closer and closer toward the edge of ecstasy.

"You're good," she murmured. "So good." She was thinking not only of the pleasure that he was giving her but of the man who was Luke Maxwell—strong and determined, loving and compassionate. With a deep sigh Jessica pulled Luke's mouth to hers and drank thirstily of his kisses. She had wondered once if she would lose him, if Mexico might be the end, and now he was beside her and this was their new beginning.

Luke's lips meandered lazily from her mouth to her cheek to the soft sensitive skin behind her ear. "You're not so bad, either," he said in a husky voice that belied the lightness of his words.

Jessica smiled and turned so that she could look down on him. His hair was tousled; his eyes were warm with desire. She wanted him very much; she'd known that for a long time. Today, she'd found out something else: she needed him as she'd never needed anyone. Soon everything would be right between them again. Very soon.

Jessica bent her head and kissed her lover, taking playful nips at his lips before she kissed his neck and slid her mouth down his shoulder and across his chest. Her hair trailed over his flesh like a soft dark waterfall while her hands found the eager hard evidence of his arousal. Luke gave a deep moan of pleasure and Jessica smiled again that she could give—as well as receive—the bounty of love.

Then his hands were lifting her up, up above him until she was astride him, absorbing his male hardness into her welcoming sweetness. They were swept away into their own world where there existed only sensation and pleasure, where nothing mattered but the pulsating need that drove them on, wild and reckless, to their ultimate release. His hot love burned inside her as they moved in rapturous rhythm, faster now, toward the moment of their shattering release, and at that moment Jessica leaned back and took him into the very core of her being, holding him there for longer than either of them could have thought possible, until they both cried out and she fell across his chest. Tears of joy stained her cheeks as Luke enfolded her, holding her tightly against his heart.

"I. . .I THINK. . ." she stammered some time later, searching for her voice and then for the words. "I think I could fall in love with you, Luke Maxwell."

"I think I've already fallen," he said.

"You do something to me. You bring out the—"

"Animal in you," he finished.

"Was I that wild?" she asked, turning shy now that she began to remember some of what had passed between them.

"Not for me," he answered with a wicked smile. "Never for me. But I must say, you were particularly passionate."

"You weren't exactly a lamb yourself." She nibbled his ear. "If I recall, you. . . ." She whispered a provocative phrase in his ear.

"My," he said. "You're making me blush. Did I really?"

"Absolutely," she confirmed with a giggle. It was calming down now, their passion, as they talked lightly about it, but both knew they'd reached heights that seemed to have been unattainable before.

"The only way for all this to end," Luke said, kissing Jessica's nose, "is with champagne—"

"And strawberries," she finished for him, snuggling comfortably in his arms. "We can dip the fat juicy strawberries into the icy champagne and then feed them to each other one by one."

Luke kissed her lips, which were no less sweet than the imagined crimson fruit. "Do you have any champagne?"

"No."

"Strawberries?"

She shook her head sadly. "But we can dream."

"Well, I need more than dreams, woman," Luke said, reaching for his glasses. "There must be something in the larder to restore my energy. After all, you just put me through quite a session. Roast-beef sandwiches? Cold chicken? Anything."

Jessica rolled over and stretched. "Let's see, there might be some wine in the fridge. And maybe a slab of cheese."

"That's it?"

"Lettuce?" she offered.

"Never mind; it's getting worse." Luke got up, pulled on his trousers and headed for the door.

"Oh, Luke, could you bring up my briefcase, too? It's in the middle of the kitchen floor."

"Briefcase? No, indeed. You're not going to work while I'm in your bed!"

"Wouldn't think of it. I have a surprise for you."

Luke raised one eyebrow in interest and disappeared down the hall.

Jessica rolled over and snuggled into the pillows, thinking about what had just happened between them, remembering deliciously, reveling in the memory, until when Luke appeared she was smiling what he called her Cheshire cat smile. Under one arm Luke had tucked a bottle of wine and under the other her briefcase. In his left hand he carried two thin-stemmed wineglasses and in his right a brightly wrapped package.

"There wasn't any cheese," he said. "Might have known."

Jessica, ignoring that, eyed the package. "For me?" She sat up and extended her hand.

"Don't be greedy, Jessica," he admonished, but he handed over the gift with a pleased look on his face. While he poured their wine, Jessica tore off the paper with curious fingers.

"A book of poems. Oh, Luke." She was surprised and touched by his gesture.

"Read the inscription," he said, sitting beside her on the bed and sipping his wine.

She opened the cover. " 'To my poet laureate . . . in

memory of Mexico.' Oh, Luke," she said again, "how did you know Yeats was my favorite?"

"He's mine, and I hoped you liked him, too. In fact, I was pretty sure you did," he added with a knowing smile as he handed her a glass of wine. "Read to me."

"Now?"

"What better time? We don't have a loaf of bread, more's the pity, but I have thou beside me. So read."

A little hesitantly, Jessica opened the book, turned to one of her favorite poems and began to read. They passed another hour this way, lazily, happily, and she almost forgot about the briefcase, but Luke remembered and handed it to her.

"Now," he said, "it's my turn. What about my surprise?"

As Jessica took the briefcase, a wicked little smile curved her lips.

"Is this a joke?" he asked, suddenly suspicious.

She shook her head mysteriously. "No, but it's something you'll find very interesting."

"Then it's not what I expected—a fascinating contract negotiation or a special MT memo with which to regale me?" he teased.

"Neither," she announced as she pulled out the magazine and passed it over to Luke. "Remember this?"

He held it in his hand with a frown and then suddenly, as if time and memory had jarred him, he looked at it again and then at Jessica and back at the magazine, holding it as if it were a bomb about to explode.

"Page forty-seven," she said helpfully.

Silently he opened the magazine. His eyes raked over the pictures; his jaw clenched; his breathing became forced. He didn't turn the page. Instead, with disgust, he gave it back to her. "Get rid of that," he demanded. He might have been speaking a foreign language; that's how strange his words sounded to Jessica.

She had expected laughter certainly, embarrassment maybe, but not this cold anger. Finally his eyes met hers and held until she was forced by their demand to close the magazine and put it on the bedside table.

She started to speak, but he beat her to it with his insistent question. "Where did you get it?" Before she could answer, he asked, "Who sent this to you, Jessica?"

"No one sent it," she hedged, suddenly afraid to explain.

"Then how did it get into your briefcase, may I ask?" Again, his eyes held hers.

She put off the question to try to explain her own reaction. "I think they're rather nice, the photographs, I mean. You look . . . well, you look very sexy and appealing. Beautiful, actually."

She picked up the magazine again and turned to his pictures. She wanted to tell him how they made her feel and to laugh with him about a time long ago when he'd posed for them, but she didn't have a chance.

Luke grabbed the magazine from her and with a furious gesture hurled it across the room where it landed with a thud behind a chair. "I said get rid of it, Jessica." He took a drink of wine and then almost as an afterthought drained the glass. Then he rephrased the question he'd already asked twice. This time he would have his answer. "How did you get it, Jessica?"

She pulled the sheet up across her breasts, suddenly feeling very vulnerable under Luke's cold anger. She remembered the naiveté with which she'd thought that together they could laugh over all this. Luke certainly wasn't laughing. Jessica took a deep breath. There was nothing left but to tell him the truth, all of it.

"One of my staff members," she began, "dug it up for me." She was ready to tell him that her plan to profile him in the pages of *Scope* had been undertaken in the heat of anger, but Luke's reaction stopped her again.

"For you? For *you*?" With those words, Luke abruptly got up, reached for his shirt and in furious haste began to finish dressing. "What exactly was this staff member going to do for you?" His voice cut like a cold blast of air through the warm room. "What were you planning—to use me for the first *Scope* centerfold? Or perhaps your plans extended to *Modern Times*. Something new, a male nude?" he asked bitterly.

"Luke, I had no idea what she'd find. I didn't even see the magazine until today. I just wanted a story and asked her to—"

"Dig," he finished. "Find whatever dirt she could in Luke Maxwell's past." He fumbled with the buttons on his shirt, trying without success to fasten them. Finally he gave up, frustrated.

"Exactly," Jessica said firmly, keeping her voice calm and facing coolly the wake of his sarcastic outburst. "After we met on your show—when you were so rude," she explained, "I asked one of my reporters to investigate you." The words sounded harsh and unfeeling even to her own ears.

"Investigate," Luke repeated. His face was wary, the face of a stranger. "Why?"

"You've already guessed." Jessica tried to stop her mounting irritation. It was over, a thing of the past. There was no point in defending her reasons so strongly. They sounded a little absurd now, anyway. So she just explained, telling him about the conversation with Monty and the assignment that resulted. "Then I got to know you—" she paused, adding weakly, "—and I put it out of my mind. . . the story."

He shook his head in disbelief, and again Jessica realized how lame her words sounded. She tried to explain. "If I did think about it at all, I'm sure I thought there would be nothing in your past I didn't already know; then in time I just forgot."

"You forgot? That is an ineffectual excuse, Jessica, when you've set about to ruin a man's career." He finally got his shirt buttoned and put on his jacket.

"I didn't know what she was going to find, Luke," Jessica reminded him.

"You could only hope," he added as he turned toward the door.

Jessica leaned forward, not bothering to reach for

the sheet that had slipped down to expose her breasts. "Luke! You're not just walking out?"

He didn't look around, but his voice carried back into the room. "No, I'm not walking out, Jessica. That's your specialty. I'll be downstairs if you want to talk."

Jessica remained sitting in the middle of the bed, trying to put into perspective what had just happened. She'd seen Luke's anger twice. The first time she'd known it was coming; today it was all the more devastating for being so unexpected. She'd anticipated laughter and gotten its opposite. He thought the story—and the pictures—would run in *Scope*. She had to convince him that would never happen.

Jessica slipped on a lightweight robe, ran a brush through her tangled hair and, barefoot, went down the steps to the kitchen.

The coffeepot was perking on the stove. Two cups were set out with a carton of milk and the sugar bowl. Luke leaned against the counter concentrating on the perking coffee.

Jessica went to him and put her arms around his waist. "Darling, I *do* want to talk," she said. Luke's muscles were stiff beneath her hands. "I had no idea you'd be so upset."

He turned away to pour the coffee.

"I thought we'd laugh about this," Jessica attempted.

"I can't laugh about a time in my life I wanted to forget. Particularly when you're the catalyst who's brought it back to haunt me."

"Aren't you being a little dramatic, Luke? I'm going to kill the story."

"Do you really think you can spike something this

hot, Jessica, when an eager reporter and her editor are sitting on the story of the year?"

"Of course I can. It's my company, and they work for me," Jessica said confidently. She took the coffee from him. It was too hot to drink. She set it on the kitchen table and looked at Luke for the first time since she'd come downstairs. His eyes were a brown so deep they reminded her of a smoldering log just before it caught fire. There was a flame there, burning just behind his eyes, and it wasn't the kind of flame she'd hoped to ignite. She wanted nothing more than to extinguish it. "You said we could talk, Luke. Let's sit down and talk about this."

"You've already explained how it happens, Jessica, how you shuffle lives like a deck of cards at your magazine."

"That's not fair, Luke. I've never done anything like this before."

"Well, you sure picked a good one to start with," he said bitterly. He hesitated and then sat down beside her.

She didn't mention that he often dealt harshly with the lives of guests on his show. This wasn't the time to expand an already sensitive issue into an all-out battle. Besides, he didn't intentionally go digging for dirt. She had. The reasons didn't matter now.

"I suppose you're curious about the circumstances, why I posed for those pictures you think are so 'beautiful.'"

She nodded. She was curious, but she'd expected they would laugh over those circumstances she now almost dreaded to hear.

"For money, Jessica," he said simply. Then he told her that he'd posed for an art class in advanced anatomy to help pay his tuition. "One of the students asked if he could do a photo session with me. Said he needed more angles to sketch from and offered me a good hourly rate, enough to pay for the rest of the semester. I did the session and never gave it another thought. Didn't see the guy again—he quit school at midterm, bound for a career that didn't require a college education, as it turned out. Six months later he sent me a copy of the magazine." Luke's mouth tightened into a thin line. He saw that she didn't fully comprehend the terrible situation that had been created by the publication of those photographs.

He tried to make her understand. "If it had been another time or even another magazine, it might have all ended differently. But there was a stricter morality then; it wasn't chic or "in" to pose for nude photographs, especially if you had serious intentions about your career. The magazine wasn't pornographic, of course. The art direction was slick; the accompanying articles supposedly of value, but basically it was a series of photographs of nude young men." His lips curled in a self-deprecating smile. "Even though I had limited funds, I considered suing, but you know how difficult it is to win that kind of long drawn-out battle. I was starting to carve a plan for my life, and a scandal like that wouldn't have advanced my career."

Luke took a sip of his coffee. "I started from the bottom, Jessica, and I knew I had a long struggle to get to the top. So I decided to do nothing. Naturally, no one I knew read the magazine, so as time went by it all faded into history. Until now." He smiled a strained half smile. "Maybe the pictures will have a little more class in the pages of *Scope*."

Jessica's voice was exasperated. "No one is going to see them, Luke. I told you that."

He shrugged. "I'm afraid it isn't that simple, Jessica." He stood as if to leave, and Jessica held out her hand to stop him. He let her hand rest on his sleeve. "I suppose I knew it would come out eventually—my checkered past. I doubt if the Board of Regents at the university will be pleased, to say nothing of Arch Wheeler. I'm the fair-haired boy. Beyond reproach."

"Wheeler doesn't know?"

Luke shook his head. "No one knows. I didn't want to have to bring it up and then spend all my time proving I wasn't some kind of moral deviant."

Jessica sipped at her coffee, but it was tepid and tasted bitter in her mouth. She thought of the years she'd spent trying to fight rumors and innuendo about her own life when there'd never even been proof of wrongdoing. The photographs of Luke—if they were used—would be tangible proof, at least to some people, of his less-than-honorable character. She thought about his well-planned career—and his future.

"If you decided to go into politics. . . ."

Luke laughed mirthlessly. "Wouldn't my opponents have a great time with that one? Can you see me trying to address the issues with the audience imagining me in the buff—or worse, convinced that I was a part of that whole disgusting world?" Luke shook his head. "That's what would be impossible to live down, Jessica, the stigma of guilt by association. Interestingly enough, at dinner last night Arch outlined his political aspirations for me. Now, neither he nor his influential friends would find me a very viable candidate. That's a dream I can kiss goodbye."

"And the present? 'Speak Out'?" Her words caught in her throat.

"We could lose some sponsors. We could lose all of them," he corrected. "And Arch Wheeler might decide I'm no longer an asset to WBS."

"I never imagined when I asked Sharon. . . ." Jessica looked at Luke, her eyes filled with regret.

"Actually, I'm relieved it happened," he said, surprising her again. He put his hand over hers and sat back down beside her. "I've always said I believed in the truth. I've certainly fought hard enough for it." He met her eyes straight on and saw the seriousness in them as she listened to him. "This part of my past had to come out some time. I was angry at you for being the one to find it, when I should have been angry at myself for trying to keep it quiet."

"It's going to stay quiet, Luke," Jessica said stubbornly. "No one is going to know. *Scope* will never run the story."

"It's out of your hands now, Jessica," Luke told her.

She shook her head. She'd set into motion the machinery that had uncovered these revelations, and she could stop it. Luke had used the journalistic term—*spike*. She would spike the story. For him.

9

JESSICA HEARD THE NOISE before she saw the sea of white signs bobbing in front of the MT office. The shouts were unintelligible in the distance, and then so loud as she approached the building that she still couldn't make out what was being yelled. Out of the corner of her eye as she shot by, Jessica saw a vividly colored blur and the impression of a mass of undulating bodies, most of them women, she judged, without slowing down to look more carefully. They usually were women. The picketing of Modern Times had become a women's cause.

Jessica sped on for three blocks before doubling back into her private parking place behind the building. On any other day she would have confronted the mob to hear their protests, mingle with them, listen and talk and—if she was lucky—disperse them with promises that she'd make sure were kept, assuming the complaints were legitimate ones. She'd handled two groups that way during her years of bringing *Modern Times* magazine into the world of the eighties. In both cases the picketers were voicing Jessica's own concerns, and she imagined they were doing so today, but at the moment her mind was on something else. Causes, even good ones, would have to wait.

That was her explanation when Toni tried to stop her headlong rush into the office, and Jessica followed it with a curt demand, "Call Monty LaBaux and tell him to come up at once."

Toni, wide-eyed, mouth still open to spill out the story of the picket line, reached obediently for the phone. This wasn't like her boss—this brusque and demanding behavior with no explanation, but the past few days had been crazy. Not so crazy, though, that she hadn't been able to get a handle on what was going on. Today she was totally perplexed. Monty LaBaux didn't fit into the picture at all, so this had to be a new problem, and from the look of Jessica Hale and her tone of voice, it was a bad one.

Within minutes, Monty had taken his place opposite Jessica's desk but Jessica wasn't behind it. She'd gotten up, walked around the desk and stood leaning against it. She needed to stand—to assert herself physically as well as psychologically for what she was about to tell Monty. She needed to get to the point quickly without mincing words; Monty wasn't the type for meaningless palaver. Still, she'd decided, when she'd rehearsed the short speech the night before and honed it on her drive to work, there was a compliment due before the bombshell could be dropped.

"I read the Maxwell story," she said. "It was a well-researched and well-written job. The girl has a good style, a flair that stands out but doesn't jar the *Scope* tone."

"Agreed," Monty said, but there was already a frown forming on his dark smooth brow. "She's a comer. And she can dig. Far and away the best investigative reporter I've got. You saw the photos in that magazine, Jessica. Apparently they've been lying dormant for a dozen years or more. They make the story."

Well, Jessica thought without surprise, he'd given her the opening right away, on purpose, she suspected. Might as well plunge in now. She was glad she'd decided to stand. Monty's authority, even seated, was considerable, and this was going to be a first. She'd never gone over his head at *Scope*.

"That, I'm afraid, is the problem. It's too inflammatory, too destructive and by far too much of a cheap shot for *Scope* or any MT publication. This is *Tattler* stuff, Monty, and I'm not going to run it."

He said nothing but sat staring at her with a look of puzzlement flickering in his black eyes; Jessica knew that his mind was racing along a thousand miles a second.

His response, when it came, was in the form of a question, unexpected. "How long have you been in charge at MT, Jessica? Two years?"

"About that," she answered, tempted to return to the sanctity of her chair behind the huge desk. She restrained herself and remained in front of Monty.

"First time you've ever used the spike, isn't it?"

"The first time and I hope the last. I don't like to do it, Monty, but remember, this story was my idea in the first place. It was poorly justified, unprofessional and, I hope, uncharacteristic. I shouldn't have started it; I shouldn't have let it drag on. I did both. Now I'm going to have to spike it."

"You also shouldn't have gone away with him considering what was going on up here, Jessica."

"How did you know about that? Toni—"

"You know better, Jessica. I just figured it out about ten seconds ago. I should have realized it when you made the assignment. For God's sake, I saw the show; I saw the electricity between you two, and I saw your reaction when he bested you. It was pure revenge with a tinge of chemistry, Jessica. Typically female—the first move you've made since I've joined MT that was made by the woman in you and not the executive in you. It was a mistake."

"I know that, Monty, and I should have stopped the story the next day or at least the next week. I simply forgot."

"Love does that," he said wryly. "But now it's too late, Jessica. You have to let it run."

"No," she almost shouted. "With the photos or without, I never would run a story about the man I—I love in one of my magazines. It would be unprofessional at best, Monty."

"Without the pictures, it would be unprofessional; with the pictures, it would be gutsy."

"Then let's just say I don't have the guts."

"You have them all right. You're just not sure he does."

Jessica didn't respond immediately. She'd never considered that, and for at least thirty seconds she let her mind dwell on it. Then she answered. "I'm more sure of Luke than of myself, Monty. This is my decision, and I've made up my mind to spike the story—for one basic reason. What Luke did was no more than a mistake of youth. The suffering he'd incur would not come from the deed itself but from the sensationalism. There're politicians in high government positions at this moment who were kicked out of college for cheating or arrested for drunk driving or worse. I find those mistakes of a much larger scale than innocently posing in the nude, but because what Luke did was so provocative, it would cause a scandal. Therefore, I choose to suppress it. Since the story was assigned to my magazine by me, that's my choice." This time, everything said, Jessica sat down.

"Sharon can take it somewhere else" was Monty's only response to all of his boss's carefully thought-out logic.

"No, she can't." Jessica spoke sharply and with authority. "She wrote that story while she was on my payroll and at my direction. Make sure she understands that, Monty, and emphasize the steps we'll take—legally—to stop her."

Monty had an answer for that but decided not to voice it. Jessica was too bright to be mollycoddled. She knew the stakes, she knew Sharon Jessup, and she was betting a real long shot, in Monty's opinion.

Jessica sensed what was on Monty's mind, and after he left her office she decided not to call Luke with the news right away. Like Monty, she knew there was to be another visitor.

The buzzer rang ten minutes later. "Sharon Jessup's out here, Jessica. I told her you had two appointments backed up and that problem downstairs, but—"

"It's okay, Toni. Send her in."

Sharon Jessup was an audacious little bundle of energy barely five feet tall with short-cropped reddish hair and a pointed face. She'd always reminded Jessica of a kitten with her slanted green eyes, which if they couldn't see in the dark could surely see far beyond the limits of most reporters. Those eyes probed and the quick mind assimilated. This was no kitten, Jessica suddenly realized, but a full-fledged jungle cat. Her back was arched, but not obviously, because Sharon knew a formidable opponent when she saw one. She skittered to the opposite side of the office and took a corner chair and waited, but she wasn't purring.

Jessica didn't bother to get up. This wasn't a difficult opponent, only a junior reporter.

"You did a fine job, Sharon, on the Maxwell story." The girl opened her mouth as if to speak and then quickly closed it like a fish gasping for air when Jessica continued without pause. "We can't ruin a man for a mistake made years ago, however, and that's why I'm killing the story."

The pink mouth had a chance then to form its words and did so quickly before it could be stopped. "That story could make *Scope*, Miss Hale, and it could make—"

"Your name," Jessica finished for her. This time she stood up, not for any psychological reasons but because she wanted to end this meeting quickly.

"We can't run a cheap sensational story just to make your name, Sharon. You're good, and if you stick with the magazine and with Monty, you'll have a fine career ahead, a distinguished career. This story would simply put you in league with the muckrakers. That's not the kind of name you need at this juncture," she advised, and hoped Sharon understood. "As for selling magazines, *Scope*'s reputation has already been established—through slow hard work, not through sensationalism."

Sharon's doubtful cat eyes shifted, and Jessica found herself continuing the explanation, which was beginning to sound like a broken record. "This story would hurt Maxwell, Sharon, and it wouldn't help you or the magazine except momentarily. When the fire of the scandal died down, you'd find yourself there in the ashes. You're a good reporter in a world that's changing fast. There're important stories out there, and I'm convinced you'll be writing the best of them. You'll get another chance—a better chance—and soon." Jessica had a feeling that if the metaphor of the ashes missed its mark, she'd possibly captured the girl with the promise, which she suspected Sharon knew was genuine. She was wrong.

Sharon stood up, green eyes turned upward toward Jessica. She was trembling, not, Jessica guessed, from fear but from rage. "There'll never be another chance like this. We can be the first with the news about Maxwell's past; we can blow New Orleans apart with my story and the pictures."

Patient until now, Jessica was irritated by that bit of bravado. Her voice was firm. "What you have written, Sharon, is a good story illustrated with some sensational pictures that aren't going to blow New Orleans or any other place apart." She paused to let her blunt words sink in. "My decision is final and irrevocable." She didn't bother to add that she was sorry. She wasn't in the least sorry for what she was doing now, only for what she'd done before.

Sharon was no fool, though, and she was beginning to see where Jessica's mistake lay. "Then why did you assign me the story in the first place? Why did you ask me to get the goods—to find out 'every intimate detail'?" Before Jessica could answer, she added, "I gave you just what you wanted and more. Now you're spiking it. Why?" Sharon challenged, her face flaming even more red than her bright hair.

Jessica walked toward the open door of the office through which she could see Toni, her mouth open again in amazement. Well, it had been an open-mouthed couple of days. But normalcy was just around the corner that she was about to usher Sharon Jessup out of, but not without an admission and a promise.

"I made a mistake, Sharon. It wasn't my first, and it won't be my last. I regret that you had to be involved in this one, but there are elements of your very fine work that we may be able to use. Monty has been building an article about the machinations of the Louisiana broadcast scene. It's very complicated and there's definitely more to it than meets the eye. You have a good start with the Maxwell research. I'm sure Monty'll want to put you on it." What she said was absolutely true while it was also obviously bait. This was the first golden ring that could be offered. There'd be others, and Jessica meant to grab a few for Sharon and, ultimately, for Luke.

She paused at the door, waiting for Sharon to join her. The young woman didn't want to leave, but Jessica knew she would. Jessica wasn't about to listen to one more word, and Sharon saw that decision in her face. She marched out the door, and resignation seemed to have replaced the fury in her tight tense little body.

Jessica glanced at Toni, who closed her mouth with effort. "One more phone call and we'll get to the picketers," Jessica assured her assistant.

"Something tells me that problem, as large as it is, will be a relief," Toni answered as Jessica turned, went back into the office and reached for the phone. Luke picked it up on the first ring as if he'd been waiting.

"It's just as I told you, darling. All taken care of."

TWO DAYS LATER, JESSICA STEPPED from her car into ninety-five-degree heat with humidity even higher, headed across the asphalt pavement and went into the hospital to wait. Hours of work, a night shared with Luke, an occasional meal, infrequent sleep—all this had been sandwiched in between the waiting ever since Crawford checked into the hospital.

Today she waited for the surgery to be over, a wait that was interminable, interrupted once briefly after two hours had elapsed. That news was brought by a young intern—she'd been too distracted to even remember his name—who told her there were complications. Because of scar tissue from the previous surgery, the time needed to get into the heart cavity had been double what the surgeons expected. The operation would be prolonged but that would not, she was assured, change the prognosis. Jessica knew better, or thought she did. At Crawford's age, the length of surgery and extended time under anesthesia were worrisome if not dangerous signs. She could understand that much, and she was terrified. She seemed to be losing control of everything and everyone.

That sensation had begun with the call in Mexico, and now even the superficial day-to-day problems seemed to have been magnified way out of proportion and merged with these important issues until at times Jessica couldn't separate the trivial from the grave. The problem with the picketers, for example, had turned out to be over an article in *Modern Times* magazine, which referred to a twenty-two-year-old woman involved in a local holdup as "the girl with the gun," the objection being that, had the gun wielder been male, he would not have been called "the boy with the gun." Jessica agreed and with irritation told the one hundred protesters that the distinction between *girl* and *woman* would be carefully made in the future, but added acidly that a letter to the editor really would have sufficed in this case.

Now here she was, waiting alone for news of Crawford. She imagined that the lobby was crowded with friends and business acquaintances and, of course, reporters, all of whom on this critical day had the courtesy to remain downstairs, but now she suddenly needed company and wished that someone would join her in this lonely vigil.

Someone did. It was Monty, and Jessica greeted him with a cry of relief before learning, only too quickly, that he had come to add yet another burden to her already laden shoulders.

"Of all the days in the world," he began after asking about the progress of the surgery, "to lay this on you, but the vultures are gathering, and I thought I should warn you so you can be prepared."

"Tell me," Jessica said woodenly. "I assume it's bad news, and waiting won't make it any easier to take." She had an idea what he'd come to tell her. She'd suspected, deep down, from the moment Sharon Jessup left her office; even when she'd called Luke and reassured him, she'd doubted her own positiveness. Now she knew there'd been reason for doubt.

Moments later, when the shock had passed—not passed, really, just settled in— Jessica realized that what she'd expected was nothing compared to what she faced.

It lay beside her on the plastic sofa in the waiting room where she and Luke had sat, a discreet few inches apart, that morning just four days earlier. Today there were no other visitors. She and Monty were alone, and he'd gone over to the water fountain, had a drink, continued on to the little balcony, taken in the dull view and returned to sit down beside her during those few moments that passed while reality sunk in.

The newspaper that he'd taken from his briefcase and put on the sofa had been recognizable immediately. It was the *Tattler*, and on its front page was Luke's picture, an edited version, but leaving no doubt that Luke Maxwell had posed without benefit of clothes. Jessica had closed her eyes quickly and then opened them to watch Monty make his circle of the little waiting room. She didn't look at the paper again or read the caption or turn the page, even though there was bound to be more on the following pages.

Monty picked up the paper and returned it to his briefcase. "Sharon went right to the *Tattler*," he said unnecessarily.

"We can sue," Jessica mumbled.

"The damage is done, Jessica. This'll die down in a few weeks. A trial would take months."

Jessica agreed. She was too upset for anger, too heartsick for revenge. She could only think of Luke and the damage he faced.

Monty reached for her hand and held it tightly. "Don't worry about Luke, Jessica. He did this to himself."

Jessica nodded. "Years ago. I just came into his life and put it all in the papers," she said with an ironic smile.

"He'll survive," Monty reminded her. "Hell, I've read his bio. The man's got nine lives like a cat. He'll land on his feet."

"He's a good man, Monty; you'd like him." Jessica seemed to have to say this; she wasn't quite sure why.

"Jessica, you love him obviously, so I have no doubt about his worth. Hell, it's taken you long enough to find a man who can live up to your expectations. You've picked a good strong one, and since you're damned strong yourself . . . ."

"There's more?"

Monty nodded. "There's definitely more. The *Tattler* went into great detail about your trying to spike the story to protect your 'lover.' That, of course, is speculation on their part, but since it's correct, you don't come out looking too good, Jessica."

She digested that latest news and then attempted a bleak smile. "I can't stop to worry about that right now."

"True. You can't even worry about Luke's problem right now. I just wanted you advised of it so you'd be prepared when you leave—when the surgery's over and Crawford pulls through. Which he will," he promised emphatically. "Do you want me to stay with you?"

She nodded and then successfully put everything—Luke's photographs, the *Tattler* story, her own involvement—out of her mind for the next long hours. Crawford's pain and suffering and his struggle for survival was uppermost now. This was life and death, and it could not wait. The other would have to wait; she just hoped that when the time came to face it, the love she and Luke shared would enable them to endure this final violent attack.

FOUR HOURS LATER, Jessica left the hospital by the circuitous route Luke had used days before while Monty LaBaux walked boldly out through the lobby to deal with the press that had collected there. She'd given him the keys to her Jaguar and taken his small sports car. It wasn't exactly inconspicuous, but neither was it recognizably hers; it would be good enough for the visit she planned.

Jessica made a quick stop at her house, changing into jeans and shirt, and then with the sun still bright in the late-afternoon sky, she drove swiftly, almost recklessly over the bridge that spanned the Mississippi. She drove with relief and something akin to hope. Relief because Crawford had come through the surgery even better than the doctor anticipated. The valve had been replaced, he was breathing on his own, and the prognosis was excellent; but through it all, she had only been able to wait, with no control over the outcome.

For what lay ahead with Luke, she could do more than sit by, and she would. The hope Jessica harbored was for what lay ahead, not as serious as life or death, only as serious as the future of the man she loved.

Jessica turned off the highway onto the narrow road that led toward Luke's house without reducing her speed, even when she saw the cars parked along the drive. She ignored them, ducked her head and sped toward the barn. Stopping Monty's car beside the caretaker's house, she gave Sam a wave and hurried through the corral gate and into the tack room. None of the reporters would have recognized Monty's car, but some might be curious enough to investigate.

Quickly Jessica reached for the saddle and bridle. A golden head peeked over the stall door to greet her. Thetis was there, but Hector was not. She'd guessed right. Luke had gone to the one place where he could be alone and safe to think. Jessica was going to him, and she'd have to hurry.

She led the cream-colored mare from the stall, slipped the bridle over her head, heaved the saddle over her back and cinched it quickly. Jessica's left foot was in the stirrup when she heard an engine, maybe more than one, starting up at the house. She swung into the saddle, glanced toward the open door, changed her mind and headed for the back of the barn. Leaning over the horse's withers, she yanked at the rusty, rarely used catch, unfastened it and gave the door a shove. Once in the open air, she dug her heels into the horse's flanks and Thetis broke into a canter. The corral fence was low. The mare took it easily and pushed her way ahead, skirting carefully through thick woods until she found the bridle path. Then Jessica urged her into a gallop.

"Come on, girl," she whispered into the wind. "We're going to Luke."

The sun was setting in a blaze of color as they sped through the woods on the little path that had been cleared for a walking trail. It was narrow and curving, splashed with streams and overhung with low branches. Jessica urged Thetis on, knowing that as a rider she was skilled enough to keep her mount from going down or herself from falling off. It was careless to push the horse so hard with branches whipping across her face and nearly catching in her hair, with turns throwing her off-balance and muddied streams to jump. She didn't care. With an impatient hand she brushed away the brambles, leaned low over the saddle and gripped with her knees until they ached. She was going to Luke.

She'd guessed right. He was at the cottage. Hector,

tethered to a tree, whinnied in welcome as Jessica jumped from the saddle, dropped the reins to the ground and ran toward the cabin.

Luke opened the door and stood looking at her. He neither spoke nor smiled. His face and eyes were as serious as Jessica had ever seen them. Hope, the same hope that had been with her since she slid behind the wheel of Monty's car, pounded in her heart. It was a hope that Luke's love was as strong as hers. It shone through the uncertainty on her face as she stood at the bottom of the four steps leading to the porch and looked up at him, not confident enough to go farther.

"I thought you'd be at the hospital." Luke made the statement in a voice that was emotionlessly flat.

"Crawford's in recovery. He's going to be all right," she added.

"I'm glad."

Jessica remained looking up at him. The space between them seemed as wide as the Mississippi. Everything in her cried out for Luke, but she couldn't climb the steps that would close the gap between them unless he wanted her to. They stood silent for what seemed an eternity. She felt the challenging sun setting hotly on the back of her neck. It seemed to prod her on. She couldn't know how Luke felt unless she asked. Determination won over trepidation, and she held out her hand.

"Will we be all right, Luke? Will we ever be all right again?"

Jessica saw him move down the steps toward her and for an instant she thought maybe it was all a dream, a mirage created by the sun that blazed from behind her, but then she was in his arms and feeling his body pressed against her, and she knew this was no dream. The tears that had glistened in her eyes spilled down her cheeks.

"It's always been right with us, Jessica," she heard him whisper. "Always." Her tears wet his face. He wiped them away and carefully pulled the leaves and thorns from her tangled hair. "God, I'm glad you came. I wanted you here, but I couldn't ask you to leave Crawford."

"I have enough love for both of you, Luke," she said softly through the tears. "More than enough."

As they climbed the stairs and went into the cabin together, Jessica knew that this day would bring a commitment that would be expressed through love-making no less tender, no less passionate, but far more permanent than ever before. With it would come the unspoken promise that they would never be parted again.

In an almost boyish frenzy, Luke circled the room, gathering pillows and throwing them into a vibrant pile in the middle of the floor. Then he pulled off his clothes; duplicating his movements, she undressed, too, and together they dropped onto their makeshift bed.

"It's like lying in a field of flowers," Jessica said. "All these radiant colors."

"None as dazzling as you," he answered, touching her gently, almost reverently, before covering her mouth with his eager kiss. "And none as bright as our love. I do love you, Jessica. Now. Always. No matter what."

"No matter what," she repeated. "You've forgiven me. . . ."

"There's nothing to forgive. A long time ago I was foolish; more recently, I was thoughtless. All my anger is gone; there's nothing left but love."

"I love you, too, Luke," she whispered, drawing his lips once more to hers. So light and airy, hers was a kiss that might have gone on forever, a kiss they might have exchanged had they really been surrounded by a field of flowers. It was an outdoor kiss that tasted of sunlight and warm breezes, that started at the corner of his lips and then moved across as she licked gently with her tongue. He waited and let the kiss come. It was her kiss, and it was frolicsome and loving. She caught his lower lip between playful teeth and then brushed against his upper lip, feeling the enticing tingly bristle. She moved her tongue slowly to trace his mouth before probing inside, retreating, returning, entwining with his waiting tongue and finally exploring deeper and deeper.

Luke let out a low husky moan, turned her on her back and returned the kiss but not so slowly, not so gently. His mouth crushed hers and his tongue invaded until she gasped for breath and ached with desire. Then and only then did the dual kiss end, the quivering bodies meet, anxious and ready.

She held him, her sun and rain, her spring and summer. Everything that was Luke was now, somehow, Jessica. His smile, his frown, his laughter, his anger, his powerful love. Everything. She could not imagine tearing herself from him, for only Luke made her come to life. Only he made her bloom. She opened to him as a flower to the sun's life-giving rays and wrapped herself around him and brought him into her and drank of his sweet nectar until they were one. His gift was the strong sun of his love, hers the flourishing blossom that accepted that love.

LATE INTO THE EVENING, they shifted as lovers do when they're entwined in the sleep that comes after their lovemaking, and opened their eyes. Luke kissed Jessica lightly and reached for his clothes. "We need to talk."

"We have the whole night," she said lazily, making no move to get up. Then she saw his surprised expression and told him, "I'm not leaving until you do. From now on we're together. A team. A duo. Twosome, pair—" she started to giggle "—twain." With that last word, she reluctantly reached for her clothes. "But I'm perfectly willing to talk," she said and pulled on her jeans.

"I have a plan you need to know about," he said seriously as he finished dressing and sat down on the sofa to put on his boots.

"Is there any coffee?" she asked, zipping her jeans and crossing barefoot toward the kitchen cabinet.

"There should be some instant, but I'll have to start a fire," he responded absently before getting on to the point of his conversation. "I'm going in to the studio tomorrow morning and I'll talk to Arch."

"Then we can still stay here for the night?" she asked over her shoulder.

"Yes, Jessica, of course, but there's a lot you don't seem to be thinking about, and we need to face it now." He crossed to her but before he could say anything else she wrapped her arms around him.

"I just want to think about you and me and us," she said as she laid her head against his chest.

"It's *us* I'm talking about. What happens to us after Arch—and the show. . . ."

"What about the show? You aren't going to resign, are you?"

"I may have no choice, but it won't happen without a fight." He managed a grim smile. "I plan to go on the air tomorrow as usual—except live, I hope—and make a clean breast of my past. Arch's credo is that every man should have a chance to defend himself. Of course, he may fire me as soon as the show's over. Or trade me to Modern Times." His smile was lighter this time.

"I'm going on TV with you," Jessica announced. "I started all this, and I need to clear up my connection with you and the pictures. The least I can do is be there beside you."

"No, Jessica. It's my past, and I have to salvage it alone. Actually," he mused, "after the first horror of seeing myself in the *Tattler*, I felt a sense of relief. It's out in the open now. No more secrets."

Jessica agreed. "No more secrets. And there's no reason for us to keep our relationship hidden, either. . . ."

"As if we could—after the *Tattler*," he reminded her.

"Then let's really give them a scoop. I want to marry you, Luke. If you won't ask, I will. Let's get married now—fly to Mexico. Then I can really face all this with you, as your wife. I have the white dress you bought me, remember?"

He pulled her close and lightly kissed her nose. "You're amazing, Jessica. I'm at the lowest ebb in my life, and you're offering to share it with me."

"For better or for worse," she said persistently.

"Jessica, come and sit down. We need to talk about this and seriously. I'm afraid you're thinking with your heart right now. Let me remind you of the facts."

"I know the facts, Luke. Because of me, those ridiculous pictures from your past are all over the papers."

"And do you realize what that can do to me—to us?"

"I suppose Arch Wheeler could fire you, if he has all that moral indignation you've imparted him with."

"There's more, Jessica. My job is in jeopardy at WBS and certainly my standing at the university. As for my political career, it's nonexistent." He paused long enough for Jessica to take in all that he was saying.

"I love you, Jessica, but love alone won't solve this. If the job at WBS goes, it's a sure bet all the rest will go, too. I have to face Wheeler—and the public—and bow to their wishes." He paused again to let Jessica think. She'd known what the consequences might be; she just hadn't wanted to face them. Now he was forcing her to.

"If I have to start over somewhere, I'll start over. I'm not afraid. But if you were my wife, I'd want you with me. Would you leave MT to begin again with me in some remote place halfway across the country? Hell, who knows where it might have to be if things go against me? Can you give it all up, Jessica? Can you?"

She started to answer, but he placed his fingers over her lips. "Wait. Don't say anything yet. You need to think about it." And she knew he was right.

10

JESSICA FELT THE DAWN'S GLOW fill her body just as she opened her eyes to its bright promise and challenge, a challenge left over from the night before. Luke knew what he had to do. Now Jessica had made up her mind. Even before the first light of morning, the decision had been made. It happened sometime during the night when she awoke to find him there beside her and realized that she wanted nothing—not wealth or fame or power—more than she wanted him to be beside her always.

Before she turned over, before he opened his eyes and reached for her and filled his arms with her warmth, she'd met the sun's bright challenge and accepted it.

Their lovemaking began the day, and it was slow, easy, relaxed, as if this was not a day that would change their lives but just another sweet and gentle morning shared by two people very much in love. She told him only part of what she'd decided, but it was the part that mattered most to both of them. She told him as they sat at the table Luke had made, drinking coffee heated over the open fire, told him in a voice frank and determined. "I've decided that I'm going with you to Montana. . . ."

He frowned, and she explained. "Or Alaska or wherever you go if the worst happens. I'm with you all the way, Luke."

He put down his coffee cup. "You're sure?"

"I've never been more sure about anything in my life."

"It may be more difficult than you think, Jessica. You're used to a certain kind of life-style. . . ."

"A person can change," she replied lightly. "Besides, I have a feeling that no matter what happens, it's going to be right for both of us."

"I hope so," he said quietly. "I know this much—it's going to be a lot easier for me to face, after this." He leaned across the table and kissed her thoroughly.

"It might be interesting in Montana. I could work for the local paper—"

"And I could be a disc jockey."

They both moaned good-naturedly, but Jessica could sense a building despair within him that she refused to let surface. She gave him a hug, another kiss, insisted that he drink his coffee and then began her spiel, the other part of the decision she'd made in the night. She still wanted to go on the show with him. She made her plea strongly. His response was not just emphatic but decisive.

"No," he said flatly. "This is my fight and I'm going to face it alone."

"You're terribly stubborn, Luke Maxwell."

He nodded. "So I've been told."

Jessica turned to put away their cups while Luke finished dressing. She was pensive, but a smile curved her lips. Luke Maxwell just might not be as smart as he thought.

They'd turned the horses into a field behind the cabin for the night, and by midmorning were beginning to wonder if they'd ever catch them. Hector, frisky with his newfound freedom, dared several times to approach, tempted by a sugar cube, but always managed to grab it with his velvety lips, turn and run before Jessica could catch him. Luke finally cornered Thetis, managed to slip the bridle on her and tie her to the fence. Jessica and Luke climbed up on the top rail beside the mare and waited.

"He'll get jealous after a while and wander over."

"Then what? We don't even have a rope to lasso him with."

Luke laughed. "Wouldn't matter. I never could use a damn lasso anyway. Couldn't even get the loop going, actually. You were an expert, of course," he said with a side glance at Jessica who nodded immodestly. She was seated comfortably on the fence, her boots hooked under the rail, chewing pensively on a piece of grass. She knew what was creeping into his mind—his thoughts about the day ahead—and she was doing everything she could to close the door on them at least for a while. And for a while she succeeded.

He looked at her lovingly, seeing her as never before, the outdoors lighting her face, the breeze catching her hair, one hand stroking absently the neck of the mare beside her. Luke watched her and loved her and let her glow fill him as it had during the night. Then that reality she'd tried to close off began to seep in. It was time for Luke to get to the station, rearrange the schedules so he could put his show on the air live, talk to Wheeler, make notes, meet with the director. It was time.

"I guess when Hector heads this way again, you'd better just jump on him, Jessica."

"Why don't you?" she asked with a broad smile, still gay, still teasing.

"Told you. I can't ride without a saddle, bridle—all the accoutrements."

"Oh, well." Hector approached curiously and just when he was close enough, Jessica stood up and leapt onto his back. The big palomino was surprised, skittish and then playful as he galloped around the field with Jessica bent over his neck, her hands caught in his mane, her knees gripping his flanks. Luke watched from the fence, admiring her skill and her style and her beauty, loving her for the way she'd helped him handle what could have been a devastating morning.

They rode to the barn through sultry air that was beginning to hint at a summer rain. Sam met them on the road and took the horses.

"Those fellers up at the house finally left, Luke. 'Round about midnight. They kept poking around and saying as how you must be somewhere hereabouts. I told them I didn't have the foggiest notion. 'Course I knew good and well y'all was down at the cabin."

Luke clapped Sam on the shoulder. "You did exactly right. Hope they didn't cause you too much trouble."

"Hell, no." Sam let loose with a squirt of tobacco toward the side of the road. "Me and the wife just went on back in to watch the TV. Told them they could hang around long as they didn't make the animals skittish. They asked me was there usually horses in the barn, and I told them they was up at the blacksmith's getting shod. Reckon they figured that's an overnight job," Sam added with a grin as he led the horses away.

Luke and Jessica headed toward the house, savoring the last peaceful time they'd share this day. A heaviness hung in the air, and in the West, storm clouds were gathering fast. As she climbed into Monty's car, it seemed to descend on her, and for the first time Jessica had an ominous feeling that everything might not go as she'd planned.

But she'd succeeded in lifting Luke's spirits and keeping them up. "Come on, Jessica, smile," he challenged. "Then get yourself home, change and go to work. Treat this like any other day—except turn on the TV at five-thirty."

"You think they'll let you do it live?"

"I'm pretty sure they will." Luke kissed her again. "I'll call you as soon as it's over."

She turned the car around while he stood in the road with his hands in blue jean pockets, smiling at her, exuding the confidence that she hoped he felt—because she was beginning to lose hers. She waved and headed up the road, watching him recede in the rearview mirror, suddenly afraid—for both of them. Luke was a stubborn man and a proud one. She couldn't bear to see him lose it all. He'd do everything possible to save himself, but—unknown to him—she was going to do her part, too.

THE RED WARNING LIGHT WAS FLASHING when Jessica finally talked the guard into letting her slip inside the studio. There were no empty seats. She stood against the back wall and listened to the electricity in the audience, a current of excitement that seemed to ignite the room. From her place in the shadows she could see and hear, but Luke would never know she was there.

Jessica wondered if, once again, Luke had managed to avert the press. They were apparent everywhere in the room, but from the general tenor of the comments she could pick out, no one had seen him. They were all guessing, the audience and the press, that Luke Maxwell would indeed host today's live telecast of "Speak Out" and that it was going to be a momentous event. The house, as usual, was packed, but monitors had been set up in smaller adjoining studios to accommodate the overflow.

The lights went down on a stage black and bare. The cameras began to roll, and then a spotlight swept across the small stage and picked up Luke Maxwell, standing alone, holding a hand mike. The audience was strangely silent, waiting and expectant, but giving no hint of its feelings. Were they for him or against him? The next hour would tell.

Luke raised the mike and began to talk. He told the story they'd been waiting for without embellishment, straightforward and truthful, outlining his days as a student, his odd jobs to meet tuition and the offer he took in innocence, which resulted in the photographs that by now everyone in the studio had seen and many had brought with them.

"I should have made all of this public long ago," he admitted. "But once a mistake is made, keeping it secret sometimes becomes more important than the mistake itself. I'm here today to answer any—and all—questions about this revelation, which I gather some of you were already aware of," he added with a hint of a smile. This sidestep into humor drew some relieved laughter from the audience.

"We're opening the phone lines—" Luke added, giving a nod to his engineer "—and of course I'll also be taking questions from you here in the studio."

Jessica realized she was holding her breath. She dared to step forward a little, out of the shadows, and look directly at him. His concentration was intense, and he didn't notice her.

The first question, wisely chosen by Luke, came from a woman who was clearly on his side.

"You were just a young man," the motherly looking woman in the front row assured him. "Why, I can imagine that I might have done the same thing myself under those circumstances." Because of her appearance, her rotund figure and sweet face, it was a comment that couldn't have been more welcome. The audience enjoyed it, and the next few remarks were clearly supportive.

As Jessica listened, she saw a movement in the back row on the far aisle. A man shifted in his seat, nervously, she thought, tugged at his ear, turned away from the stage and glanced around the audience. It was Arch Wheeler, unannounced, watching and measuring.

Luke remained onstage while several pages roamed the audience with microphones, taking comment after comment, most of them encouraging. "We all have to make a living," one young man declared, his face earnest under straw-blond hair. "You didn't actually hurt anyone."

But the first few phone calls weren't so kind; in fact, they were adamant in their unwillingness to forget—or forgive—the criticism directed more at Luke's hidden past than the circumstances of the photographs. These were the comments Jessica had feared, and they came in a barrage.

"We've always trusted you," the first disembodied voice announced over the phone line. "We knew other people in powerful positions often faked us and tricked us. Many of them have been on 'Speak Out' and you've caught them in their own lies."

"I guess we're just disappointed," another caller declared, "that you're like the rest of them, Luke. Disappointed," the voice repeated, "more than anything else."

The arguments accelerated after that call, and a near-battle ensued in the audience between Luke's supporters and detractors, with the former slowly but surely getting more attention, more encouragement, even some applause. Jessica was reminded of a jury room when the tone slowly begins to shift as more and more of the jurors side with the first few who've opted for innocence.

Then came the call she'd dreaded but expected.

"All of us have something in our past that we don't want revealed, or at least not published in the paper, but what concerns me is your collusion—and I can't think of another word—with Jessica Hale from Modern Times. Sounds like the two of you conspired somehow to keep the story out of the press."

"That's right!" someone in the audience shouted, as one of the pages rushed toward the voice with his mike. "That's right," the man repeated. "Another reporter got wind of the story and told the truth. Least, it seems that way to me."

Jessica could feel the audience's mood not exactly shift, but certainly hesitate and wonder. She also felt Luke's reaction so deep down inside her it made her hurt.

His words were firm when he answered, almost harsh. "There'll be no discussion about Jessica Hale today. This issue revolves around me—"

But a woman in the audience wasn't to be daunted. Jumping to her feet quickly, she spoke up. "It seems to me that . . . that . . . woman has it in for you. If not, why'd she dig up the story to begin with? That's what happened. It says so right here," she added, flashing her well-thumbed copy of the *Tattler*, as if it were the Holy Word, for everyone to see.

Before Luke could answer, Jessica left her shadowed corner and headed down the center aisle toward the stage. She had on the same green silk dress she'd worn when she appeared on the show those many long months ago, in that other lifetime before she got to know the man onstage and made him her whole life.

Just as she reached the steps, a klieg light hit her—well planned by the director in the control booth, who hadn't had an afternoon quite like this one since the last time he'd turned his cameras on Jessica Hale.

"I can speak for 'that woman,'" she said calmly, taking her place beside Luke. "I'm Jessica Hale. I ordered the story and I killed it."

Luke reached out as if to stop her, and Jessica responded by catching his hand and holding it in a way that was both intimate and dependent—she needed to gain strength from him. He gave it to her, the strength and the love she needed; it flowed from his body to hers, powerfully. She was confident standing beside him, and she was proud.

"In a way," she said quietly but firmly, "Luke and I made the same mistake: he by not admitting the existence of the photographs from the beginning, and I by not running the story. I could give you many excuses, such as the offense wasn't worth all this publicity, and so on, all sound legitimate reasons for doing what I did. But the real reason is: I couldn't bear to hurt the man I loved."

A knowing murmur ran through the audience. Without a thought for manipulation, Jessica had struck a sympathetic chord, one she would never have found had she been searching this crowded studio for something to assure Luke of its approval. This might not be enough, but it was more than she'd expected.

"What happens now," she continued, "is up to you—the public—and to our employers, Crawford Dillon and Arch Wheeler. . . ." As she spoke Jessica noticed that Wheeler stood up and slipped quietly out the side door. She grasped Luke's hand even tighter. Deserted by Wheeler, they still had each other, and they'd make it.

"As much as we'll respect their decisions," she went on, "they won't stop us—or at least me—from our future plans. I've asked Luke Maxwell to marry me, and I'm still waiting for his answer." She turned and smiled at Luke, a smile of humor, challenge and even defiance.

Luke paused dramatically. He was honest, yes, but he was no fool, and he had a sense of timing, innate but honed to perfection on television. Luke Maxwell had always known how to use the tool of TV. Jessica wasn't surprised at the pause.

"Well?" someone in the front row challenged, playing into Luke's hands. "What's your answer, Luke?"

Luke put his arm around Jessica, but he didn't bend down to kiss her as the audience would have liked. There were some things too personal for television, too important. He did answer, though, simply, "You heard it on TV."

Even as the show ended with applause and cheers, even as they knew they'd convinced one small handful of the people in the country, they still couldn't predict their future.

Jessica and Luke left through the stage door. They didn't stop to talk to the staff or the reporters or the fans who had clustered around in those few minutes after the cameras stopped rolling, but headed straight for Luke's car, which was parked strategically nearby. Within seconds they had pulled out onto Canal Street and were heading toward the hospital. A driving rain, which had begun during the show, was still pouring down, and Jessica saw the reporters running through the deluge to their cars.

"We'll lose them," Luke assured her. "I doubt if they'll guess where we're going."

Jessica huddled beside him, damp and still unsure. "Did I do wrong—coming on the show like that—after you told me not to?"

"You did exactly right. Never listen to my advice again," Luke said with a grin. "By the way, I don't think I ever really answered your proposal."

"You *were* rather evasive."

Luke, his eyes still on the road, squinting through the rain, pulled Jessica beside him, placed his hand behind her head and brought her lips close enough to kiss without taking his eyes from the road. "The answer is yes." Then he added thoughtfully, "It could all be over at WBS, you know that, don't you, Jessica?"

"Yes, I saw him walk out," she said sadly.

"And you're still committed to our future?"

"Of course I am, Luke. More than ever." She reached over and placed her hand on his knee, and her touch was enough for him. They belonged together.

Hand in hand they hurried down the hospital corridor. Jessica pushed open the door to Crawford's room and then stopped with an audible gasp. Behind her, Luke stared over her shoulder in equal amazement.

Arch Wheeler was solidly ensconced in the chair by Crawford's bed. "Thought I'd stop by and tell your boss what happened," Wheeler said to Jessica in an offhand manner, acknowledging her briefly with a nod, as if they'd known each other all their lives when, in fact, they'd never met. "'Course, I might have known he'd commandeered a TV and seen the whole thing himself. 'You can't keep an ornery man down' is the adage I'll supply for him since he's a little under the weather."

Crawford moaned audibly while Luke and Jessica remained, wordless, in the doorway watching him. He was propped up in bed, obviously weak but with the brio still there, the panache, as he waved them in.

"We've been conversing, or at least I have," Wheeler continued as Jessica and Luke edged into the room. "Taking advantage of my first chance ever to outtalk Crawford Dillon. Got a couple of renegade employees on our hands, we both agreed. First thing we've agreed on in twenty years."

"First thing we've *said* to each other in twenty years," Crawford amended. His voice was hoarse but plainly understood.

Jessica and Luke laughed and crossed to the foot of Crawford's bed. They still held hands, like two young lovers before their mentors, but the surprise remained in their faces. They couldn't believe what was happening. The older men were having some problems with it, too.

"We figured that we still don't have a lot in common," Wheeler admitted. "But we've got you two, a couple of real pluses, and we've decided to keep you." He hesitated. Wheeler, like his television protégé, had some sense of the dramatic. "But with the stern admonishment that you never repress the truth again."

A grumble arose from the bed. "He means never kill a good story again!"

This time Luke and Jessica laughed as much in relief as in amusement. It was all over, their ordeal, and not only had they survived it, but they'd brought together the two men who'd been more than fathers to each of them. Luke's arm tightened around Jessica's waist. "Maybe those two philosophies could be compatible," he suggested.

Wheeler scratched his chin. Dillon shook his head.

"Probably not," Wheeler commented, "but we'll leave it open to discussion."

"Well, we're not leaving our plans open to discussion. Jessica's asked me to marry her—"

"Crawford tells me I missed that bit of good TV timing," Wheeler remarked.

"It was more than that," Jessica put in. "We *are* getting married."

"Tomorrow," Luke said.

"In Mexico," Jessica added.

"She already has her wedding dress."

Dillon raised his hand to stop the cheerful outbursts, but he did so with a grin, turning to Wheeler to voice their joint reaction.

"Guess you're going to be requesting a honeymoon," Wheeler begrudged. "We've talked that over, too, and settled on forty-eight hours."

Dillon nodded as Luke put his arm around Jessica and headed for the door.

"This time you're both wrong," Luke called out. He and Jessica paused in the doorway, their eyes resting fondly on the two men who'd meant so much to them. Luke gazed down at the woman he loved. "This honeymoon is going to last a lifetime."

Introducing
Harlequin
Intrigue
Because
romance
can be quite
an adventure
Available wherever paperbacks are sol
INT-5
Watch for the Harlequin Intrigue Sweepstakes.
You could win a romantic Cunard Cruise for two!
No purchase necessary. Void where prohibited by law.

Available in November wherever paperback books are sold, or send your name, address and zip or postal code, along with a check or money order for $4.25 (includes 75¢ postage and handling), payable to **Harlequin Reader Service**, to:

Harlequin Reader Service

In the U.S.
P.O. Box 52040,
Phoenix, AZ 85072-2040

In Canada
P.O. Box 2800, Postal Station A,
5170 Yonge Street,
Willowdale, Ont. M2N 5T5

DW-A-2

BARBARA DELINSKY
Fingerprints
ırly Quinn is a
oman with a past.
ırn Robyn Hart, she
as forced to don a new
entity when her intensive
vestigation of an arson-ring
sulted in a photographer's death
ıd threats against her life.
an Cornell's entrance into her life
as a gradual one. The handsome
wyer's interest was piqued, and then
ıptivated, by the mysterious Carly—a
oman of soaring passions and a
cret past.
ailable wherever paperbacks books are sold, or send your
ıme, address and zip or postal code, along with a check or
oney order for $4.25 (includes 75¢ postage and handling)
ıyable to Harlequin Reader Service, to:
rlequin Reader Service
the U.S.: P.O. Box 52040, Phoenix, AZ 85072-2040
Canada: P.O. Box 2800, Postal Station "A", 5170 Yonge Street,
llowdale, Ont. M2N 5T5
FP-2